Loved

by a

SEAL

HOT SEALS

Cat Johnson

ISBN-978-1515145707
ISBN-1515145700

CHAPTER ONE

A man didn't appreciate something until he had to go without it for a while.

Brody Cassidy knew that to be true with bone-deep certainty because he'd gone without many things for a good long while. Six months and three days to be exact, give or take a few hours . . . not that he was counting.

As he stepped off the transport and felt the breeze of the Virginia evening blow across his skin he made a mental note of all he'd missed and all he wanted to take advantage of now he was back on U.S. soil.

First, he was going to take the longest, hottest shower in the history of modern man.

And his bed—how he had missed his own mattress every time he'd lay down on his uncomfortable rack to try to sleep. Going to bed tonight on the two thousand dollar support mattress he'd splurged on last year was going to be so good he was almost giddy at the thought.

Of course that would be *after* he went out and got himself a nice stiff drink because alcohol was one of two more things that he really enjoyed but hadn't had in six months. Brody was definitely going to partake in both of those things before he lay down his head tonight.

Alcohol was one. The other was a woman. He'd gone so long without the sweet touch of one of those he was starting to dream about it—when he slept deeply enough to dream that was.

But before all of that he had to eat, because good food was right up there at the top of the list of things he missed most on these long ass deployments to some foreign country that never failed to make a man extra grateful to be an American.

Good ol' downhome cooking. He missed it. All of it, from juicy corn on the cob straight from the field to anything fried as long as it was fresh and hot and crunchy.

He'd give his left nut for Nana's fried catfish. Or her chicken and dumplings.

And God, her Johnny cakes . . . or even better, her black skillet cornbread. How much would he give for some of that right now?

Crap. Now his mouth was watering and there was no hope of getting the kind of chow he wanted in the near future.

Or was there?

As Brody hoisted his pack over his left shoulder he pulled out his cell phone with his right hand and powered it on.

Years of experience and some smart advanced

planning on his part meant he'd anticipated his homecoming and had acted accordingly. Before his unit had moved out of Turkey, while he still had access to secure computers and internet, he'd arranged to have his cellular service turned back on.

During the time away he'd used his cell phone for not much more than taking pictures and playing word games. Oh, and the device made a hell of an alarm clock too, since it seemed he was always working odd hours and having to wake up at times no man's body was used to.

After six months Brody would finally be able to use his cell as an actual phone again. He sure as hell was going to use it now as it was intended—to call his older brother Chris.

With any luck he could arrange some home cooked grub to celebrate being back. His brother always had been fairly good in the kitchen—at least better than Brody—but since Chris's retirement from the Navy a couple of years ago, he had expanded his culinary skills enough that at least they didn't have to eat take-out every night.

It wouldn't be Nana's chicken-fried steak, but Chris could definitely grill a mean bone-in rib eye and he was pretty good at frying up onions and baking potatoes. That was one of Chris's favorite meals to make.

Brody supposed a man had to do something to occupy his mind after retirement but after living the adrenaline-fueled life of being a member of the teams, how could wielding a chopping knife rather than a sniper's rifle be all that satisfying?

He couldn't comprehend it but God willing he

wouldn't have to deal with retired life for a good long while.

The future was a far distant worry. His immediate concern was food. Why eat take-out when he could have some home cooking and give his brother something to do?

He swiped through his list of contacts until he found Chris's name and then hit to make the call.

Brody listened to the ringing through the line as he crossed the tarmac, heading for the bus that would carry him to the base. When the call went to voicemail, he had to wonder what the hell Chris was up to that he couldn't answer the damn phone.

It wasn't as if Chris's only brother had been away in some foreign hellhole training Syrian rebels how to fight ISIS for the past six months or anything.

With a snort of sarcasm, Brody waited for Chris's outgoing message to end before he said into the cell, "Bro, it's me. I'm back. Where the hell you at? I gotta check in at base and stow my gear but after that I wanted to see if we could do dinner. Call me back. Bye."

He hit to disconnect and scowled.

Chris was probably balls-deep in Darci and that's why he hadn't answered. After six months of going without that particular pleasure himself the thought didn't make Brody feel all that understanding.

He sighed and shoved the cell back into one of the cargo pockets in the leg of his tactical pants just as his teammate Thom Grande trotted up beside him.

Brody shot the man a sideways glance as he showed no sign of slowing down his pace. "Hey, Thom! You anxious to get somewhere?"

Thom let out a short laugh. "Oh, yeah. I gotta dump my shit and go. Ginny flew down from Connecticut. She's waiting on me at the hotel."

Ah yes, the girlfriend. No wonder Thom was in a hurry, but his rushing to the bus wouldn't get them to base any sooner. Not when the rest of the unit still had to deplane and load onto the vehicle with all their bags.

Brody didn't bother reminding Thom of that. Instead he pushed down what felt a bit like envy and said, "Have fun."

"No doubt about that." Thom grinned and then strode on ahead.

"Where's he off to?" Rocky caught up to Brody and watched alongside him as Thom took off at a run to the bus.

"Girlfriend."

Rocky snorted out a laugh. "If she's not hiding out on that bus, he's got a bit of a wait until he sees her."

"You got that right." Grateful that Rocky didn't have a girl waiting on him, Brody glanced in his direction. "You got plans for tonight?"

"Yup. Sure do. Shower, food and then a little loving from some lucky female." Rocky had held up his hand and counted the three priorities off on his fingers, starting with his thumb.

Rocky was a man after Brody's own heart. Those were pretty much his plans too, but he had one more addition. A nice cold one to wash down that food.

There was one destination Brody knew he could get the things they both wanted. "Wanna eat quick and then hit the strip club?"

Chris hadn't answered his phone and honestly it would be easier for Brody to decompress with one of the team for a few hours than be with his blissfully happy, retired brother.

"Hell yeah. Wanna head over as soon as we dump off our shit? I was gonna shower at the base. Do you have to go home first?" Rocky's enthusiasm to get going was no surprise. He had been through the same shitty six months Brody had.

Brody shook his head. "Nope. I've always got clean clothes in my locker. But shit, my truck's at my house."

"My truck's parked on base. I'll drive us over to the club. I can drop you home later if you want."

"A'ight. Sounds good. Thanks."

It was funny how sometimes teammates, especially after a long deployment, felt more like family than actual blood relatives did.

"No problem. The guy who lives next to me in the bachelor barracks has been running my truck once a week. You know, to keep the fluids circulating and the tires from getting flat spots, so it should be good to go."

Chris was supposedly doing the same thing with Brody's truck. He only hoped his brother wasn't so into playing the happy couple with Darci that he'd forgotten about it.

With Brody's luck he'd go home to a dead battery. If that happened, Brody was going to enjoy torturing Chris for his negligence for a good long while.

Rocky dumped his pack on the ground next to the luggage hatch under the bus and reached up to scratch his beard. It had gotten pretty long while they'd been gone.

Brody hated facial hair himself. All it did was itch and make him feel hot and dirty.

Rocky was the opposite. Since he'd joined the team about a year ago, Rocky had sported a beard in some form or another. Sometimes he kept it cropped short and neat. Other times he'd grow it so long he looked more Afghani than American, which wasn't a bad thing for a SEAL.

Brody eyed the length of it now, definitely on the longer side than usual. "You gonna trim that thing now that we're back?"

Shaving was the first thing on Brody's list, right along with a shower. Now that fresh razor blades and hot water were readily available, he couldn't wait to be clean-shaven on a daily basis again.

Rocky stroked his facial hair like a man would caress his lover. "No way. Chicks love my beard."

Brody cocked up one brow. "Do they?"

"Hell yeah." Rocky snorted. "You'll see tonight."

Tonight they'd be at a strip club where it was the girls' job to pretend they loved everything about the male patrons, so Brody wasn't convinced that would be a real good test of Rocky's theory.

He laughed. "A'ight. If you say so."

"Eh, you don't know what you're missing."

"Yeah, I do and you can have it." Brody knew exactly what he was missing not having a beard and that was mostly needing to clean food out of his facial hair after he ate.

Rocky lifted his shoulder in a half-shrug. "All right. More girls for me then."

Brody had to chuckle. For tonight he wasn't worried about Rocky's threat. Where they were going, all he had to do was stop at the ATM for some cash and his evening's female companionship would be guaranteed.

Brody had to consider that. Had he become such a jaded son of a bitch he would rather pay for female attention than look for some kind of meaningful relationship?

He supposed he had.

Hell, just that term—*meaningful relationship*—had him wanting to run and hide.

Though, it was more likely he was simply being a realist. He'd done the whole love and girlfriend thing once long ago. All that experience had accomplished was prove to him that things were easier this way.

Looking for Ms. Right Now was so much simpler than trying to find Mrs. Right and then discovering later she was oh so wrong.

The number of divorces he saw in the military was proof of that.

He'd thought he found her once—the girl he might be able to spend a lifetime with—but that hadn't worked out so great.

Ashley Reed. His first love. Hell, his first for everything.

Christ, how could just thinking her name after a decade raise the memory of that teenage heartbreak all over again? That right there was reason enough to not repeat the mistake of getting involved seriously with a woman.

He rubbed at the tightness in his chest and hoped that it was just indigestion.

It had to be from the shit meal he'd eaten on the transport because he refused to admit one woman could still have a hold on him after ten years.

CHAPTER TWO

"Ashley?"

"Yes, Miss Eleanor?" Stopping midway down the hall, Ashley popped her head around the doorframe.

"Come and sit with me."

There were dishes in the sink from lunch and laundry in the dryer that needed to be sorted and folded, but what Eleanor Cassidy, the octogenarian matron of the Cassidy family, asked for she expected to get. And Ashley, nothing more than the hired help, wasn't about to argue.

"Yes, ma'am." She moved all the way into the room and sat.

"See if that television program I like is on yet."

"Sure." After close to three months of being this woman's daily companion, she didn't have to ask what show that was. Ashley reached for the remote control and switched to the station.

Being back here again, ten years after she'd left, was surreal. She certainly had come full circle.

She'd gone to nursing school shortly after high school, where she'd graduated at the top of her class, but yet here she was, working in almost the same job her grandmother had held for half her life.

The only difference was that Nana had changed baby diapers for the Cassidy family while Ashley was changing the adult variety.

But it made sense on so many levels to take this job. When Ashley's pride stung for taking what felt like a step backward in her life and her career, she tried to remember that.

She had been working the grueling night shift at the emergency room at a hospital in a city two hours away when old Mrs. Cassidy's health took a turn for the worse.

That had been a few months ago, about the same time her grandmother had taken a spill and broke her wrist.

Ashley needed to be with Nana.

More than that, she wanted to be. Her one regret about her job and her career had been living apart from the woman who'd raised her.

It made sense to quit the job at the hospital, move back in with Nana, and become Miss Eleanor's private nurse, but the job entailed so much more than nursing.

The woman might be old, but she still liked to eat, so Ashley cooked her meals during the day. And while she was there, she kept the house straight and did laundry, because really she'd be bored to death if she didn't do something. A person could only watch television so many hours a day.

Still it seemed like a giant leap backward. Her grandmother was the hardest working woman she'd ever known. And being a housekeeper was an honorable profession. It just wasn't Ashley's profession.

Before she'd had to retire because of her own health, Nana had been everything to the Cassidys. Nanny to Brody and Chris. Cook and housekeeper to the whole family, all so Brody and Chris's parents—Miss June and Mr. Howard as she'd grown up calling them—could work in their own careers.

Her grandmother had raised Ashley right alongside the Cassidy boys. Nana would bring Ashley to work with her when she wasn't in school. Where else could she have gone as a child? The Cassidys didn't mind. One of the perks of the job, she supposed.

The older lady stared at her through cloudy eyes and smiled. "So pretty. But then again you always were, even as a child. I always told that grandmother of yours she'd better keep an eye out or the boys would be all over you."

Ashley swallowed hard remembering how only one boy had been all over her and little did Miss Eleanor know it had been her then eighteen-year old grandson Brody. He was the boy Ashley had loved from the moment she realized boys were for more than just being annoying and teasing her.

Not that Brody had teased her all that much. Chris sure had though, as if he'd been her older brother, instead of just Brody's.

Uncomfortable with all the memories and the secrets she'd kept from this woman Ashley fidgeted in her chair.

She'd purposely kept the fact she and Brody had gotten closer, much closer, from Miss Eleanor.

The woman was old school in every sense of the word. No way in hell would she have been happy with Brody dating the help's granddaughter.

Not that the Cassidys were rich. They weren't.

They were working middle class living in a lovely but modest three-bedroom home, but the fact remained her family worked for their family.

To a woman born in the 1930s in Alabama, the granddaughter of their housekeeper dating Brody would have been completely unacceptable.

At least, that's what Ashley believed, then and now.

It had been the reason that made her keep their relationship secret, but it wasn't the main thing that kept her from running away to be with him on the East Coast after he'd joined the Navy.

Her motivation for that had been different.

If she had followed him when he'd asked, she knew she would never have gone to nursing school as planned. If she had managed to be his wife and go to school at the same time, what were the chances she would have graduated, and with honors?

It might have been too easy to step into the role of wife and mother even if it meant sacrificing her own aspirations. It had been too huge of a decision, and too scary of a move, to make at eighteen years old.

No surprise she'd chosen the familiar over the unknown and stayed in Alabama to attend school.

Letting him go had cut her deep. Him too, she knew, judging by his anger then and the fact they hadn't spoken since.

It was a regret she'd hold on to until the day she died. Even so, she wasn't sure she'd make a different choice now.

After being lost deep in her thoughts for a long moment, Ashley realized she was being rude. The older woman had given her a very sweet compliment, if in a bit of a backhanded way, and she needed to accept it graciously.

"Thank you, ma'am." Ashley ran her hand over her hair and noticed some of it had escaped from the tight bun.

There was no way to avoid the frizz. It overtook her hair in this weather.

It was late September but in Alabama, the heat and humidity still wreaked havoc with her hair.

Impossible hair was a legacy she'd inherited from her grandmother's side of the family, along with the woman's tall stature and long limbs.

Ashley supposed that, in a kind of mixed blessing, she'd gotten the Cassidy family from her grandmother too.

For better or worse, she'd accept the gift graciously, just like her grandmother had taught her to. But deep down, every turn of a corner raised memories of a past she wished she could keep buried in the deep recesses of her mind because thinking of Brody, what was, what might have been, never failed to cause the pain of a knife in her heart.

CHAPTER THREE

Over his years in the SEALs, Brody had stowed his kit after short missions and also after long deployments.

He'd done it enough times he could secure his shit in his sleep. In fact, he'd come home so exhausted from some missions it's possible he might have actually done that a time or two.

Today he wasn't tired. Nope. Quite the opposite. This evening he was revved up and ready to go.

He finished stashing his gear in the caged shelves quick enough and then locked the gate behind him. There his stuff would stay, safe and ready to go until the next training or mission came around.

Brody headed to the showers and in spite of his immense enjoyment of the luxury of scalding hot water and kick ass water pressure, he made short work of showering and shaving.

He had places to go and women to see.

Apparently Rocky was in as much of a hurry to get moving as Brody. The man strode out of the shower room and into the hallway leading toward the locker room just after Brody did.

Now that he was clean, Brody was ready to eat. He waited for Rocky to catch up to him down the hallway and said, "Hey, you in the mood for ribs? There's that place right next to the club."

Rocky's eyes widened at the suggestion. "Oh God. Ribs."

Brody laughed at Rocky's groan. "I guess that's a yes?"

"Yes. Dude, perfect idea."

"A'ight. Sounds good." Brody grinned, happy with his plans since Chris had never bothered to call him back.

With the evening plans set, they walked through the door of the locker room, Brody first, and Rocky directly behind him.

When Brody stopped in the doorway, Rocky walked smack into his back.

"What the hell are you—" Rocky stopped his bitching the moment he looked past Brody and saw what had halted him dead in his tracks.

Mack stood in front of Speedy's locker, obviously in the process of emptying it out.

With a feeling of dread twisting his gut, Brody swallowed away the lump in his throat and stepped farther into the room. "Mack?"

Mack turned, his eyes sunken and dark as his gaze met Brody's. He answered the unspoken question with the shake of his head.

"Christ." Rocky blew out a breath. "How?"

"Sniper." That was the only word Mack spoke before going back to filling the brown cardboard box.

"Shit." Brody watched as the last of the man's belongings were transferred.

Mack turned away from the empty locker and stared into the box. "That's everything. All he's left behind. Doesn't even fill half a damn cardboard box."

Silently, Brody was thinking pretty much the same thing as what Mack had voiced aloud.

Speedy and Brody might as well be the same guy. No wife. No kids. No girlfriend even. Both completely focused on work and when not at work, focused on play.

But what did that leave behind?

When his corpse was rotting in the ground beneath a cold slab of stone with his name chiseled on it, what would he have left that would last?

Half a box full of junk that nobody's gonna want.

Yeah, Chris would put it on a shelf somewhere, or he'd deliver it to their momma and she would cry over it for a while, but that would be it. It was still just a box full of crap.

"You still wanna go out?" Rocky asked softly.

"Yeah." Now more than ever. "Maybe skip the ribs and go right to the club?"

"Good idea." Rocky pressed his palm to his stomach, probably feeling as sick as Brody.

Mack glanced up. "Where you going?"

"Strip club. Wanna come?" Brody asked, not

wanting to exclude Mack but not sure he was up for going out.

Mack let out a huff of breath tinged with a humorless laugh. "Yeah, actually, I do."

Brody figured they all needed the same thing right about now . . . a reminder that even though Speedy was gone, they were still alive.

Rocky drove Brody over in his truck while Mack followed behind on his motorcycle. They should have taken one vehicle. Chances were good they'd all be too shitfaced to drive home later anyway.

Odds were also good that after losing his teammate Mack would be drinking heaviest of all. More than he should if he was going to get on that bike later.

Too late to change the plans now. They were already at the club by the time Brody considered the foolishness of the transportation arrangements.

Luckily the number for the cab company was taped to the phone on the bar and probably programmed into every one of their cell phones. They'd use it if they needed it. Plenty of vehicles were left at the club overnight after the driver had a few too many. That would be nothing new.

Brody waited for Rocky to pull the truck into a spot and cut the engine before he unbuckled his seat belt and swung the passenger door open.

They were there early, not that time had any meaning inside the club with its blacked out windows and perpetually dim interior. There'd be girls riding the poles from noon until closing time.

All being there early in the evening meant was that it wasn't packed inside yet. They found a table off to the side where they could still see the stage but be away from the few guys already planted up front ogling the girls.

"I got first round." Brody headed directly for the bar, not waiting to hear what the others wanted. There was only one drink appropriate to toast their lost friend.

He leaned against the bar as the burly male bartender, who could easily double as a bouncer, came over. "What can I get for you?"

"Scotch. Single malt. Oldest you got. Three, straight up."

The bartender wore a sympathetic gaze as he took in what was likely a grim expression on Brody's face. The man had probably figured out this was not some bachelor party or celebration.

He nodded and moved to get the drinks.

Tending bar at a club right outside the back gate of the base, the man had probably seen quite a few sailors here toasting fallen brothers.

He returned with not three but four glasses and the bottle. He poured two, lifting one in the air himself as he waited.

Brody lifted the other filled glass. When the bartender downed the shot, Brody did the same.

The man put his glass under the bar and proceeded to fill the three glasses. "This round's on the house."

It was a kind gesture, but Brody could only guess this shit wasn't cheap. "Thanks, but I don't want you to get in trouble—"

He reached for his wallet as a gruff laugh answered his protest.

"I won't get in trouble. I own this place. And before that I served my twenty years. I know that look on your face. I've seen it before. Hell, I've worn it myself. Let me buy you guys this round. Give the girls a nice tip before you leave tonight and we'll call it even."

Brody didn't argue with him. "Thank you. I appreciate it. So when did you buy the club? I'm here a lot and I've never seen you."

"Guess it's been about six months now." His bushy brows drew low. "Can't say I've ever seen you here before though."

Obviously a lot could change in six months. Brody drew in a breath. "Yeah, well, I haven't been around for awhile."

"Gotcha." The owner pushed the filled glasses forward.

Brody grabbed two in one hand and one in the other. "Thanks again."

The man tipped his head and then moved to take care of a barely clad waitress who'd come up to the bar.

As the bass pounded through the sound system, Brody made his way across the floor, dodging tables and chairs until he reached their spot.

There he planted the glasses down with a clunk. "On the house. The new owner's a veteran."

Rocky raised a brow. "Nice."

Mack didn't say anything as he reached for the glass nearest him.

Any loss, no matter which team, hit all SEALs hard, but this one was hitting Mack hardest.

Brody had known Speedy and liked him. They'd

gone through Green Team training together so he
knew him pretty well, but they weren't as close as
Mack and Speedy had been from serving in the
same unit. Brody didn't feel the responsibility that
he saw weighing on Mack's shoulders.

That feeling that he could have done something
to prevent it. That it could have easily been him
instead.

There but for the grace of God go I.

They all knew that to be true.

Brody raised his glass. "To Speedy."

"To Speedy." Rocky and Mack echoed the toast,
and then there were three empty glasses on the
table.

The cocktail waitress, trained to notice these
things, was there in seconds. "Another round?"

Not of scotch or he'd be under the table. "Beer
for me." Brody turned to his two companions.
"Rocky?"

"Beer for me too."

"Mack?"

Mack nodded.

"Three beers." Brody stood and wrestled his
wallet out of his pocket. He pulled out his credit
card and tossed it on her tray. He was saving his
cash for other purposes. "Put it on that."

"You got it."

They waited in silence. Brody knew to give
Mack time and space. They were there if he needed
to talk. They'd still be there if he didn't want to.

In the meantime, life went on around them.

The song changed and so did the dancer. A
brunette replaced the bleach blonde on stage, her

sequined G-string a different color than the last girl's had been, but aside from hair and costume the girls were pretty much interchangeable.

So it would go, all day and until the wee hours of the night.

"My father had emailed and said he needed to talk to me." Mack's words brought Brody's attention back to his friends. "We arranged a time for a phone call. We had trouble getting a clear line so I was running late. We'd just gotten on when I was scheduled to go out. Speedy volunteered to go out with the first truck and said I could follow in the second one, to give me a few more minutes."

"Where were you guys?" Rocky asked. "We've been gone so long I didn't even know you were OCONUS."

The waitress took that moment to appear with their order. They had to wait for Mack's answer as Brody took the time to add a tip and sign the credit card receipt.

Once the waitress was gone again, Mack reached for one of the beers and took a long swallow.

"We were trying to take back fucking Fallujah." Mack kept his voice low as he spoke. Brody and Rocky leaned in to hear him. "As if enough blood wasn't shed the first time, now we have to go fight to get it back. The problem is it feels like fucking ISIS is better organized than the Iraqi army we left in charge when we pulled out."

Brody let out a sigh at the truth of what Mack said. It did feel like ISIS had the upper hand. Not just organizationally, but they didn't have to play by the rules like the U.S. troops did.

ISIS triumphed by using fear and perpetrating crimes against humanity. Killing the males of the villages they raided. Selling the females, even young girls, as sex slaves to be raped repeatedly by their new *owners*. Preaching a religious doctrine that, no matter how crazy it sounded to a Westerner's ear, seemed to get them an unending supply of followers and fighters. Young, fresh and angry men, ready to kill and die for a cause Brody doubted some of them even understood completely.

"I'm sorry, man." Rocky leaned forward, his hands clasped on the table around his beer. "But you can't blame yourself because of your dad's phone call."

"I don't. I blame the bastard behind that scope." Mack blew out a breath and then tipped his bottle back, draining a good portion of it. "Still, it was supposed to be me. Not him."

The brunette was still doing her thing up on stage as they sat contemplating their mortality. Or maybe just their beer.

Hell, a man in his line of work could only think so long about the fact they could, and most likely would, be hurt or killed in the line of duty.

Eventually you had to move on to other thoughts or it could drive you crazy.

A cute stripper he'd never seen before moved across the floor, eyeballing their group. Brody made eye contact. She smiled and he nodded.

He downed the last of his beer and stood. "I'm heading to the back room for a bit."

"A little soon in the evening for that, no?" Rocky lifted a brow.

"It's been six months. So no, it ain't too soon at all." Brody lifted his chin in Mack's direction. "You gonna be here when I get back?"

Mack glanced up and Brody saw the weariness beneath what looked like anger. Not anger at Brody, but more likely at all the other people involved. At the sniper for making the shot. At his dad for requesting that call. Even at Speedy for taking the bullet and leaving Mack with the guilt of being a survivor while his friend was dead in his place.

Every one of Mack's emotions made complete sense to Brody, but still there was nothing he could do about any of them.

"I'll probably head out right after I finish this." Mack held up his beer. "Thanks for buying, man."

"Anytime." God willing next time the occasion would be a happy one. Brody glanced at Rocky. "I'll be right back."

Rocky grinned. "I'll be here so don't rush on account of me."

Brody had no intention of rushing, but after six months of being deprived, his body might have other ideas.

The dancer sidled up closer and looked up at Brody as he stood over her. "Private dance?"

"Yes, ma'am."

He looked her over. Her hair was blond, though judging by her complexion that was from a bottle, not nature.

Tall but curvy with big brilliant eyes, she reminded him enough of his one and only serious relationship that he should know better than to go in back with her.

Letting a stripper who brought to mind the only girl who'd ever gotten beneath his skin get him off was pretty messed up, but Brody had never claimed to be otherwise.

He'd come in with enough cash that in exchange she should be willing to make him forget the name of any other girl he'd ever been with.

Hell, hopefully for a big enough tip she'd make him forget his own name for a little while too.

CHAPTER FOUR

"Why is no one else out tonight?" Brody glanced around the club and didn't know a soul, save for Rocky.

Not that he could muster the energy to care all that much. The blonde had left him feeling boneless—no pun intended. At the moment it was all he could do to lift his beer.

"No clue. Isn't it Friday?" Rocky asked.

Brody thought about it for a moment. They'd cooled their heels at the transit center in Romania on the way home from Turkey for how many days? Two maybe?

Right when he was feeling happy and relaxed, the question was making his brain work too hard to calculate what day it was.

Brody decided it would be easier to go about this another way. "Hey, darlin'?"

"Yeah, sweetie?" The woman smiled extra wide

as she sidled closer to him and rested her hand on his shoulder.

She should be extra sweet to him after the fistful of twenties he'd given her in the back room.

"What day is it?"

"You mean like the date?"

"No, not the date. The day of the week. Is today Friday?"

"Yeah, it's Friday." She laughed. "Where you been? Living in a hole or something?"

Rocky snorted at the truth of her statement. *Hole* was as good a description as any for where they'd been.

A bare bones training camp in Turkey. A hole. Same thing.

"Yup. Pretty much." Brody raised his beer to her in a toast and answered her for both of them. "Thank you much for the clarification though. I appreciate it."

As for the girl's smart mouth and comment, since she'd used that mouth damn well in the back room, Brody figured he could forgive pretty much anything that came out of it now.

She sashayed away and Brody watched the sway of her hips until she was out of sight.

Shaking his head he blew out a breath. One time in the back wasn't going to make up for the six-month long drought, but it was a start.

He turned back to Rocky. "So, apparently it is Friday."

Rocky grinned as if he knew exactly what thoughts had caused the lag in Brody's return to the conversation.

"Apparently. And as you said before, where the hell is everybody else? I don't know a soul in here."

The guys from his returning unit who had wives and girlfriends and kids would be with them. But Brody could only guess where his civilian friends were. "At the bar, maybe? Now that the guys are all pussy whipped, they can't be going to strip clubs anymore or they'll get shit from their women."

"It's a hell of a thing, getting put on lockdown just because you're dating a girl. I mean no touching and no fucking other girls is understandable, but even looking is off limits?" Rocky shook his head. "You can keep that shit."

Brody didn't have much of an opinion on the matter since he didn't have, and didn't intend on getting, a girlfriend anytime soon.

He picked up his cell phone. "I'm gonna track those motherfuckers down and tell them to get their sorry asses over here."

"Yeah. You do that." Rocky nodded enthusiastically, his voice a bit louder than necessary to be heard over the music.

The beer had been flowing for a couple of hours now and Brody was starting to suspect they'd both be too drunk to drive anytime tonight.

Calling the guys to meet them would serve more than one purpose. Besides getting the guys out of the house on a Friday night, Chris could be the designated driver and save him and Rocky from having to take cabs home.

Brody sent out a group text figuring that was the most efficient. Besides, he was too lazy and bleary eyed to text them all individually. He sent the message off to Jon, Zane, Chris and Rick. At least one of them had to be around.

He put the phone on the table and eyed the action on the pole.

With his squeeze from the backroom now on stage performing, Brody felt the need to watch her gyrate. He was so engrossed it took him a few minutes to realize nobody had gotten back to him.

Frowning, Brody picked up the cell and looked at the readout to make sure. "What the hell?"

Rocky turned from watching the dancer. "What's up?"

"Nobody texted me back." Brody held up the blank screen of the phone as proof.

"Is there something going on we don't know about?"

"Hell if I know. Maybe." Brody lifted one shoulder.

The guys he'd texted were all civilians now but that didn't mean they couldn't be away on an operation of their own.

Since leaving the Navy, each in his own time and for his own reasons, they'd become private military contractors. All four men were now involved in some way with Jon's brainchild, Guardian Angel Protection Services.

Maybe there was something happening at GAPS that Chris hadn't told Brody about. Chris hadn't known Brody would be home today, only that his unit was en route.

Chris would know as well as anyone that transit could take anywhere from days, to weeks, depending on weather and other shit.

Brody decided he'd try his old CO Grant Milton. Maybe he knew something. Hell, maybe he'd even come out and meet them for a beer.

Grant was married, but Brody had been away for half a damn year. The man's wife had been married to a SEAL for long enough she should understand that sometimes guys needed to get together, just the guys.

Since texting hadn't worked out too well for him so far tonight, Brody decided to try to call. Over the din of the music pumping out of the sound system in time to the female strutting on the stage, he listened to the ringing on the line, before he heard Grant's voice.

"Brody."

"Hey, Grant."

"Haven't heard your voice in a while . . . and what is that God awful noise in the background?"

Brody laughed. "I think it's a Miley Cyrus song actually. I'm at the strip club."

"So you're home. Chris didn't mention it last time I talked to him."

"I am home and he didn't mention it because he didn't know. We just hit the tarmac a few hours ago."

"Well, welcome back. Sounds like you went right to celebrating your homecoming, so that's good. Don't waste any time, do you?"

"Nope. That's one of the reasons I'm calling you. I thought some of the guys might want to meet us. I texted pretty much all of them and got no reply. You have any idea where they're at?"

"Oh, you wouldn't know if you were in transit.

GAPS got called out on a mission."

"A mission? All four of them?"

"Actually, just three of them. I think Rick's away with that actress girlfriend of his. He's running her security now that she's working on a new movie up in New York."

New York? Brody frowned, not sure he'd heard Grant right over the pumping bass. "Wait, what about Rick's job here in Virginia at the nuclear plant?"

"He gave notice and quit that job."

"When?"

"Hell, I don't know. Let me think. Almost a month ago now, I guess it was. I know he was talking about putting in his two weeks' notice when I saw him at the party at the new GAPS office."

What the hell? Brody couldn't keep up with the shit Grant had dumped on him in just the past minute and he could only put a small part of the blame for that on the booze. It seemed as if everything had changed.

"What new GAPS office?"

"Jon finally gave in to Zane's bitching, bit the bullet and spent some of the company's money. They're renting a space for GAPS to work out of now. Man, you have been out of touch."

"I've been a little busy, but yeah, it sounds like I missed out on quite a bit." Brody shook his head at all that Grant had revealed. "So why don't you meet me and Rocky here and catch us up on things?"

Grant hesitated for long enough that Brody braced himself for the eventual excuse. His wife wouldn't like it or some version of a lie to cover that truth.

"All right. The club out the back gate?"

"Yup. That's the one." Shocked Grant was actually going to come, Brody managed to answer.

"I'll see you in a few."

"A'ight. See you." Brody cut the call and glanced up at Rocky. "Grant's coming."

"You're old CO?" Rocky asked. He'd joined the team after Grant had already moved into a training position.

"Yeah. I'm kinda shocked. He'd come out with us all the time when he was single but he hasn't made a habit of coming here since he got married a couple of years ago."

Rocky wobbled his head. "Maybe there's trouble in paradise."

Brody drew in a breath and let it out. Everything else had changed since he'd been gone, so why wouldn't Grant's marriage have as well?

Apparently GAPS had gone from holding meetings around Jon or Rick's dining room table, to renting legit office space.

Rick had quit his job and was dating and traveling with an Academy Award winning actress who also happened to be the sexiest woman alive, at least according to one magazine last year.

Chris was going to have some explaining to do when he got back from wherever the hell he'd gone off to on this three-man GAPS mission.

He could have at least let Brody know what was happening. Then again, Brody hadn't been all that diligent about phoning home.

He'd try to call home at least once a month to

keep his momma and grandmother happy, and Chris when he had a chance, but more often than not calls home fell by the wayside.

In Brody's defense, he had been a little busy . . . and that was exactly the problem. It was too easy to let this job consume all else in life.

His schedule had been grueling over the past six months. Sometimes it was just easier to not have to put on a happy face for the folks back home. They wouldn't understand. Not like the guys who he was there with.

Brody realized that if he didn't watch himself the time could come when he'd have nothing but the job left. Then when his end came, whenever that might be, his entire legacy from a lifetime of fighting bad guys all over the globe would fit inside a cardboard box, just like Speedy's had.

What a depressing thought that was.

He blew out a breath and glanced up to see Rocky's gaze pinned to the stage, a stupid grin on his face as he watched one of the girls strip off another piece of her costume.

It seemed Brody was alone in this metaphysical crisis.

"I'm thinking about going home."

Rocky's head whipped around at that statement. "Now? Your CO is on his way here."

Rocky had misunderstood Brody's out of the blue statement. Why would he rush home tonight? Chris wouldn't be there. There was no one to miss him if he strolled in at sunrise or not at all.

"No, not now. I mean take leave and go home to Alabama for a visit. It's been a while since I've seen the family."

"Sure. Why not? You got the time saved up. As long as there's no big shit on the horizon we don't know about, I don't see why the head shed wouldn't let you go."

"Yeah, that's what I figure." It was the perfect time to ask for leave. What hard ass commander would deny a man a trip to visit his momma after he'd been deployed for six months?

It would be good to be home for a little while. It might help him remember what he was fighting for.

Of course that was a double-edged sword because he'd also be reminded of what he'd sacrificed so he could be in that fight.

What he'd left behind and who—

Grant came through the door before Brody had time to finish his beer or his thought.

Standing, Brody extended his hand to shake Grant's. "Hey, that was fast."

Grant lived in officer housing on base so he was close by, but Brody had figured it would take him some time to convince his wife he had somewhere he needed to be this late on a Friday night.

Grant tipped his head to the side. "Eh, it makes things easier when the wife just stops talking to you completely."

Things made more sense to him after that comment. Maybe Rocky's guess about Grant's possible marriage troubles was correct.

No surprise there. There was some insane statistic floating around that close to ninety-percent of all SEAL marriages failed.

Whoever kept track of that shit sure had a shit

job.

"Do you know Rocky?"

"I know *of* him, but don't think we've ever had the pleasure." Grant extended his hand to Rocky, who stood and shook it.

"Know of me, huh?" Rocky shot Brody a sideways glance. "Should I be worried?"

Brody lifted one shoulder. "Now that Grant's an instructor, unless you're planning on going back and starting your DEVGRU training all over again, I guess it doesn't matter."

Grant smiled. "All good things, I assure you. And actually, I put in a request to move back over to the teams."

Brody widened his eyes at that. "No shit? You're quitting the instructor gig? I figured you'd ride out that cake walk until retirement."

"Yeah, so did my wife. That's the problem. We don't exactly see eye to eye about my decision." Sitting in the empty chair that Mack had occupied, Grant glanced around them. "Where's a waitress?"

Rocky stood again. "I gotta take a piss. I'll find her and send her over."

"Thanks. Appreciate it." Grant looked weary and like he could use a drink as he leaned back in his chair. His eyes barely flicked to the girl on stage before he turned his attention to Brody. "Good to see you back. And in one piece."

"Yeah, no shit. You hear about Speedy?"

Grant drew in a breath. "Yeah. News like that travels fast. Even to us instructors who are back here safe in the rear."

Brody shook his head. "It's bullshit. Dying over

the same city we fought for only a decade ago."

"I know. We shouldn't have pulled out of Iraq. It was too soon. They weren't ready."

"Same damn thing is gonna happen in Afghanistan."

"Most like." Grant let out a breath. "That's one reason I want to come back. I've been there. I know this enemy. ISIS might be the new favorite story in the press, but there is nothing new about them. The media talks about all the young men they're recruiting, but they've got a sophisticated hierarchy. The leadership of that organization is populated by experienced fighters. Men who've already faced us. Hell, some we trained ourselves. And make no mistake, they are organized and damn well too."

"Which is why there's all those drone strikes to hit the key leaders." Brody nodded.

"The leadership decapitation strategy doesn't work. These bastards plan for the losses. They have members ready to step into any leadership vacancies. It's set up like the U.S. government. Anything happens to the President the Vice President is trained and ready to take over. If he goes, there's the Speaker of the House. But unlike the U.S., whoever takes over for a fallen—and don't forget martyred—leader will only be more vicious. More vengeful. It's better not to give them a death to rally around."

"And the devil you know is better than the devil you don't know."

"That can be true as well." Grant sighed and glanced around them again. "Is this the waitress?"

Brody swiveled his head and spotted the blonde

he'd spent some quality time alone with tonight. "Nope, but for what I tipped her in the back room, I reckon she'll carry over a couple of drinks for us if I ask real nice. Hey, darlin'!"

As the girl made her way through the thickening crowd toward their table, Grant snorted out a laugh. "I think I didn't appreciate my single days quite as much as you do."

"No doubt." Brody shot him a grin.

It was one of the sad truths of life that a person didn't usually appreciate what they had until it was gone. That was exactly why Brody was putting in for leave and, if he got permission, would be driving to Alabama to see his family.

It was also the reason he might let this pretty young thing sit in his lap one more time tonight.

He could always make more money. What he couldn't make any more of was time and none of them knew how much of that they had left.

CHAPTER FIVE

"Brody's here." The older woman's voice brought Ashley out of her own thoughts as she concentrated on putting away the clean clothes she'd just folded from the dryer.

Miss Eleanor wasn't healthy but the old woman had retained her wits. At least, until now.

"No, Miss Eleanor. Remember, Brody is in Virginia."

"He might have been, but he's here now."

Ashley turned to the old lady, concerned this dementia was a new symptom, when she noticed the woman smiling and staring out the window.

With her heart pounding and a feeling of dread mingled with crazy anticipation, Ashley swiveled to face the window.

Damned if there wasn't a truck parked in the driveway. She hadn't seen him in a very long time, and even though he was now a man of almost thirty and not a kid anymore, she had no problem recognizing him immediately.

She might be old and ailing, but Miss Eleanor was right. Brody was back . . . and what the hell was Ashley going to do now?

Hiding in the closet came to mind. It certainly seemed simpler than facing the man after their last confrontation. Him angry. Her crying. Both of them too young to be dealing with the feelings and the decisions they had wrestled with.

It was as if it had all happened yesterday instead of many years ago.

One thing she knew for sure, she couldn't have their first time seeing each other again be under the overly observant eye of his grandmother.

Ashley was no good at hiding her feelings, which is why she'd hid completely from the woman's sight all those months she and Brody had been together. It had seemed like the only way to avoid Miss Eleanor seeing right through her.

That was probably still true now.

She jumped up from her seat. "I'll go let him in."

"Girl, that front door has never been locked in all the years I've lived here. Besides, nobody has to let Brody in. This is still his home, even if he is traipsing around the world half the time."

"I know, but it won't be a very nice homecoming for him to walk into what looks like an empty house. He won't know to come back to find us here in the bedroom in the middle of the day."

"You're right. It's a thoughtful idea. You go greet him. The boy deserves that much. Besides, I don't want him scared that you've locked me up here in my bedroom like an invalid even though I'm perfectly fine. You'll want to give him some warning about that."

"Yes, ma'am." Ashley didn't have time for the debate of whether Miss Eleanor was really bedridden or not.

Brody was here and Ashley would be lucky if she could get her legs to walk her to the door, forget about argue with a crafty eighty-year-old.

She strode through the bedroom door, fast before Miss Eleanor could think of anything more to delay her.

In the hallway, Ashley picked up the pace to a jog as she headed for the front door just as a shadow loomed behind the frosted glass.

It would be so much better to have this reunion outside instead of in the foyer where Miss Eleanor might hear everything.

Diving for the knob, Ashley pulled the door open just as Brody had reached a hand out to do it himself.

He stood there, wide-eyed and with a duffle bag in one hand indicating he was planning on staying for at least a little while.

Her chest tight, she managed to squeak out, "Hello, Brody."

Brody's mind spun. With observations, memories, questions . . . the biggest question being what the hell was Ashley doing opening the front door of his parents' house?

She flushed with what he could only guess was surprise at seeing him for the first time in a decade.

Damn, how could she look even better than he remembered?

More, how could he ever have compared her to that stripper the other night? Now, in the light of day, face to face with the reality of Ashley rather than just the memory, there was no comparison.

Her light hazel, flecked with green and gold eyes were the same as they'd always been, he was sure, but after having not seen her for so long, he was struck again with their brilliance.

She had her dark hair pulled back tight but the tendrils that had escaped to curl around her face reminded him how she'd so often left it loose and wild when they were younger. He'd loved the carefree look on her then.

And her body—ten years had only added to the curves he'd found so completely irresistible back then.

As his groin tightened as much as his chest at the sight of her, he realized nothing had changed in that department. The memories of being with her were still strong and that fact alone pissed him off.

"Ashley." He had nothing else to say yet at the same time unasked questions swirled in his brain.

"Um, I didn't know you were coming." She sounded as uncomfortable with their meeting as he felt.

Again he had to wonder what she was doing there and why were they standing outside in the Alabama heat with the door open rather than going inside? He could feel the cool air-conditioned air escaping past her.

As she continued to stand in the doorway,

essentially blocking his way, he figured the only thing to do was answer her. "I didn't know I was coming myself until my command approved it. I figured I'd surprise everyone."

Only he hadn't known *everyone* would include the girl he'd lost his virginity to. The same one who'd broken his heart.

Damn. It turned out that he was the one surprised.

She nodded, her gaze dropping to the military issue three-day pack with his last name embroidered on the tape.

If she hadn't known and had been wondering if he was still in the military, his mention of his command and his pack should have confirmed it for her. His enlisting all those years ago had been what had broken them up.

Nothing had changed . . . He was still in the Navy. She would no doubt still not approve of that. So why was he envisioning backing her up and taking her against the wall? Taking her so hard neither of them would ever forget it.

Did he want to hurt her like she'd hurt him? Or just remind her how much they'd loved each other before she'd destroyed it?

Hate was as strong as love, he supposed.

That thought gave him pause. Did he hate her?

No, he didn't, but the hurt and anger and resentment still lived inside him, even after all this time. He'd never had true closure.

Maybe this overwhelming craving to possess her was simply because in spite of the traumatic end to their relationship, Ashley felt like home to him—as

much as this house and his family did. That
sensation, at a time when he really needed to feel as
if he had a home and a family, was pretty powerful.

With Speedy's death, and Chris still away and
without communications on whatever this
mysterious GAPS mission was, Brody was feeling
more out of sorts than he usually did.

Coming home from deployment was always an
adjustment, but with nothing and no one to greet
him after six months away but a couple of strippers
and an empty apartment, Brody needed to feel
something familiar.

For better or worse, Ashley was familiar, even if
they'd lived like strangers for the past decade. And
she was here, right in front of him, still acting as if
she didn't want him in his own house.

"Uh, can I come in?" he asked.

Her eyes widened. "Oh, of course. I'm sorry. I
just wanted to meet you here and warn you."

Warn him? Good lord, what now? He couldn't
take much more upheaval. "Warn me about what?"

She cringed at the hard tone even he had heard in
his own voice. "Nothing horrible. It's just your
grandmother's health isn't what it used to be so she
stays in her bedroom mostly. That's why I'm here.
To help while your parents are at work all day."

"Where's Nana?" Brody asked.

He felt ill at the thought something had happened
to the woman who'd raised him and Chris, even if
she was Ashley's grandmother and not his own.

"She's okay but she had to stop working. She's
up there in years herself and when she fell and
broke her wrist—"

"And nobody bothered to tell me any of this?" Brody let out a string of cusses that he shouldn't have in front of any lady, or anyone else besides one of his team, but he couldn't help it.

Just when he'd been depending on the stability of family, he'd come back to find his nice stable home life had been turned upside down while he'd been deployed.

Chris was gone to God only knew where. His grandmother was so ill she needed a caretaker. Nana was hurt and had quit the job she'd held for forty years.

What other nasty little surprises awaited him?

Ashley's touch on his arm brought his attention back to her. "You were away. They didn't want to worry you. And honestly they're both fine."

He pulled his arm back far enough she had to drop her hand. If he couldn't have her the way he wanted to, he'd rather she didn't touch him at all. He couldn't take it right now.

"So what? You're the housekeeper now?"

The girl who'd had such big plans for her life. College. Career. Plans for a future that were too important for her to risk putting them in jeopardy by coming with him to wherever the Navy chose to send him.

Anger flashed in her eyes. "No, I'm not the housekeeper and what would be wrong with it if I was? My grandmother is the most honest, hardworking—"

"Stop. I apologize. I didn't mean it like that. It's just all a shock."

Her being here was like a sucker punch to the gut

when he'd already been against the ropes and fighting to stay upright.

She drew in a deep breath. "I'm a nurse. I left a good job at the leading hospital in Alabama to come here to help because Nana and your family needed me. I'm here all day with Miss Eleanor while your parents are at work, then I go home to Nana every night."

Whether Brody liked it or not, Ashley was about as close to being a part of his family as she could get without being an actual blood relative. While he'd been halfway around the world defending the freedoms of strangers, she'd been here taking care of his loved ones.

Pissed at her or not, how could he not feel grateful to her for that?

Speedy's death was proof that a man had to settle his affairs when he had the chance because he didn't know when there'd be no more time left.

Brody pushed down the anger he felt at her over the past. While he was at it, he did his best to bury the guilt and anger he directed toward himself for being away for so long and so often when a good son would be here where he was needed.

Holding on to anger had worn on him. He realized that now as the weariness and sheer exhaustion hit him all at once, like when the adrenaline rush wore off and he crashed hard after an op.

Time to make amends. At least be civil and honest. "I'm glad you're here, Ashley."

She lifted her dark brows. "You are?"

He didn't have any fight or strength left in him.

Hell, at this point he was happy he was still standing.

"Yeah, I am." Dropping his duffle to the ground, he gave up trying to resist the urge to grab a hold of the familiar, the comfortable, what he knew. What he'd loved. He reeled her in with one arm and squeezed her hard.

He leaned his chin on her head and inhaled the familiar scent of her. It transported him back a decade and all the emotions hit him full force. The good, the bad and everything in between.

When he'd decided to come home, he hadn't bargained for all this.

Pulling back, he drew in a breath to steady himself. "Is my grandmother awake? Can I see her?"

"Oh, God, yes. Of course. Sorry. She's in her room." Ashley stumbled back a step and cleared the doorway for him to enter.

He grabbed his duffle again and stepped into the cool of the house.

As he closed the front door behind him, he took some satisfaction that she looked as off kilter as he did. All after what amounted to just a hug between two childhood friends who had, for a short time, been so much more to each other.

It might be petty of him, but he was happy this reunion hadn't been any easier for her than it had been on him.

Which raised the question, why? Were there still some feelings on her end? Regret maybe?

What the hell was he doing even thinking that? Even a tiny glimmer of hope would open him up for a world of hurt.

Even so, he couldn't help himself as his gaze dropped to her left hand. He saw it was bare of any rings.

Damned if that knowledge didn't have his pulse picking up speed, which only made him pissed at himself and her.

Been there, done that.

He and Ashley were over and had been for a long time. Now that circumstances had put her back in his life, he'd work to keep things friendly. Nothing more.

The logical part of his brain was on board with that plan, but damned if the rest of him didn't have other ideas.

He watched the sway of her hips as she led the way down the hall of his childhood home and decided he liked how the years had filled out her figure.

Thoughts like that were dangerous. He was already feeling like an emotional, hormonal teenager again. He wasn't sure if that stemmed from visceral memories of the past, or a sign he'd needed to take some time off more than he'd realized.

In any case, his relaxing trip had turned into one hell of an emotional roller coaster and there was nothing he could do besides buckle up and hang on tight. He only hoped he'd eventually start to enjoy the ride because right now, the way his stomach churned like he was upside down in a loop and about to lose his lunch, it could go either way.

And just when he was already thrown off his game, he had to paste on a smile and get ready to lie to his grandmother—possibly the shrewdest, toughest, hardest woman he'd ever known.

"Grandmother. How are you feeling?" Brody left his bag on the floor and stepped into the room.

Eleanor Cassidy wasn't a *nana*, or a *memaw* or even a *grandma*. She was most certainly *Grandmother* to Brody and Chris, and referred to respectfully as Miss Eleanor by most folks around town.

Taking her hands in his, Brody leaned down and pressed a kiss to her wrinkled cheek, before sitting in the chair next to the bed.

The old woman was thinner than he remembered, making her skin sag a bit more around her face. Her complexion seemed more sallow, as well.

In spite of those indications of her failing health, there was still a strong flash of attitude in the glare she directed at Ashley as she said, "I'm perfectly fine and there is no reason for this one here to keep me confined to my room."

In light of the feistiness he saw in his grandmother, Brody had to wonder if that were true. He shot a glance at Ashley. She had her lips pressed tight, looking as if she wasn't about to get into an argument about the subject.

He had a feeling he'd stumbled upon a long standing debate regarding the details of his grandmother's care. "Well, maybe now that I'm here I can help you outside and we can sit on the front porch for a bit."

Her grey brows drew low. "Sit outside in the heat? Don't be ridiculous."

That would teach him to keep his bright ideas to himself.

Brody got a renewed appreciation for exactly how hard Ashley's duties were, being here all day, every day, alone with his grandmother.

"It's been a long time since we've seen you." There was no question in his grandmother's statement, but he felt the need to answer anyway.

"I know. I apologize. I've been out of the country for a while."

She pursed her lips. "You'd think those politicians and generals could come up with a better plan than tearing young men away from their families and sending them God only knows where. There are plenty of convicts taking up space in prison on the taxpayers' dollar. They should send them instead."

As he squelched his opinion regarding the absurdity of her idea, Brody nodded. "Yup, there sure are. But I don't make the rules, Grandmother. I just follow them."

"Well, at least you're here now. How long are you staying?"

He braced himself for her reaction. Whatever he said, it wouldn't be long enough in her opinion. The truth was, he'd been lucky to get as much time off as he had. Even so, command could recall him at any moment.

"If I don't get called back in before, I won't have to leave until Sunday afternoon."

"Good. You'll attend church with me Sunday morning. If I'm allowed to go, that is." She shot Ashley another accusatory look. "Ashley, have you offered Brody some sweet tea?"

"No, ma'am. Not yet." Ashley turned to him. "Can I get you something to drink?"

Nurses must be trained to deal with difficult patients, because Ashley didn't even flinch at his grandmother treating her like she was a servant rather than a highly skilled health care professional.

"Sure. I'll come and help you." Brody stood.

He wasn't about to let his ex-girlfriend wait on him in his own home. Besides all the personal stuff, she was a nurse, not a waitress, and he was able to get a drink for himself just fine.

"The girl is perfectly capable of handling two glasses of tea, Brody."

"I'm sure she is, but you raised me to be a gentleman and I'd like to help." He led the way into the hallway before his grandmother could make more of a fuss.

It wasn't until they were in the kitchen that Ashley spoke. "Miss Eleanor was right, you know. You didn't have to help. I could have handled two glasses of tea."

"Well, it goes without saying that Miss Eleanor is always right. And it's three glasses because you're going to sit with us. You're not the housekeeper."

"You mean like my grandmother was? No, I'm not." It was clear from her tone she was insulted.

Brody leveled his gaze at her. "That's not what I meant and you know it."

After a pause, she drew in a breath. "I know. You just have to realize, I've changed, the whole world's changed, but to Miss Eleanor, as far as social niceties go. . ."

"It might as well still be fifty years ago." He finished her sentence for her.

"Exactly."

He watched as she moved to the cabinet and took down two glasses. He took a step forward and reached for a third glass, placing it pointedly on the counter next to the other two. "Did she always treat you and Nana like you were—"

"The help?" She glanced over her shoulder at him as she reached for the pitcher of tea on the counter. "That's exactly what we were."

As a kid, he had been too wrapped up in his own life, and later when he was a teenager, in trying to find more ways to spend time alone with Ashley, to have noticed.

It wasn't until now he realized the full impact of what she'd probably felt all those years ago. That his grandmother had been raised in an age when, in her mind, he and Ashley shouldn't be together.

Being employed by his family didn't make Nana, and shouldn't make Ashley, second-class citizens. As if they were lesser, but it probably had and he just didn't notice.

Nana was simply the woman who had raised him.

Now, he had to wonder at Ashley's motivation for everything. Her insistence no one ever know they were secretly dating. Even her breaking up with him took on a whole new light.

All these years he'd assumed her decision had come from a place of selfishness. Had she been worried about being accepted by his family because of her family's position in their lives?

In the absence of the anger and resentment he hadn't realized he'd been holding on to, some empathy had room to begin to creep in. He reached out and brushed a hand across her cheek.

When that one move startled her and had her drawing back he realized how distant the time was when she'd wanted him to—had expected him to touch her.

He pulled his hand away. "I'm sorry you have to deal with all this."

"Brody, it's my job and I've handled patients who were much worse. Believe me." She smiled and it actually looked genuine.

She didn't understand he was talking about so much more than his grandmother being a difficult patient.

When he remained quiet, unsure of what to say, she tipped her head to one side. "Are you okay?"

That one question, delivered with the concern of a friend and nothing more, shouldn't have twisted his gut, but it did.

He didn't know what came over him, but before he knew it, he found himself spilling his guts to her. "We lost a guy."

"Brody. I'm sorry."

He nodded his acceptance of her sympathy and kept talking. "That's why I wasn't here earlier. I stayed in Virginia for the memorial service."

She reached out and laid her hand on his arm and he decided he was tired. Tired of thinking. Of fighting.

That one gentle touch did him in. He reached out

and pulled her against him for the second time that day.

Ashley wrapped her arms around his waist. He squeezed her tighter in response.

What the hell was it about this woman that made him need to hold her? Was it just the memory of the girl who'd been his friend for years before she'd been his first and only love?

Maybe it didn't matter why.

All that seemed to matter was that holding her made him feel better. Grounded. Home.

She pulled back a few inches and raised the same eyes he used to get lost in to meet his. "Is there anything I can do?"

"Yeah. There is." He moved in closer before he thought better of it.

Before he talked himself out of the urge he wasn't sure he could control anyway, he crashed his mouth into hers.

When she didn't pull away, when she kissed him back, there was no more thinking. He let his mind shut down.

Brody refused to think anymore and just let himself feel. Feel her. Feel safe. Feel home.

Bringing one hand up he cradled her head while holding her body tightly to his with the other. When he breached her lips with his tongue, the soft sound of need she let out stole his breath. He forgot where he was as kissing her blocked out all reason.

"Brody?" The distant sound of his grandmother's summons penetrated the surreal haze.

He broke the kiss but didn't let her go. Instead he leaned his forehead against hers and waited for his heart to stop pounding.

"We should get back to her."

"I know." Still Brody didn't move. Not to let go of her. Not to go to his grandmother even though he knew he should.

She tipped her head so her gaze could find his. "I thought you hated me."

He let out a breath tinged with a laugh. "So did I. Turns out I was wrong."

Her breath had quickened with the kiss, just like his had. There was no way either one of them was going to move on and forget this had happened. He figured he might as well accept that. "Stay with me tonight."

Her eyes widened. "What?"

"Stay here. For dinner. For longer."

"Brody—"

"What are you two doing in there?" His grandmother's question interrupted Ashley's protest.

"We'll be right there. I had to fix more tea," Ashley called back, providing a viable excuse that Brody wasn't sure he would have been able to come up with on his own.

"I told you that you need to make a fresh batch every day or we run out!"

His grandmother obviously had no problem issuing orders while bedridden.

"Yes, ma'am." Ashley's eyes remained on his even as she called the answer to his grandmother, before she lowered her voice to answer his question. "I have to go home to Nana. We have dinner together every night and then watch TV."

She moved to pull back and he held tighter. "Then come back. After Nana goes to bed, meet me."

Ashley would know where. As teens they'd both snuck out of their houses enough times to be together.

A crease marred her pretty brow. "I don't know—"

"Please."

Ashley drew in a breath. "Maybe. Now, let me pour this dang tea and get it to Miss Eleanor. She's fixin' to pitch a fit if I don't."

"Okay." He released her, but it was with a smile on his face as he did it.

Gone was Ashley's mature professional persona that he'd found so strange and jarring since he'd found her at the door. Back was the girl he remembered. The one who said *fixin'* and would do anything she could to avoid disappointing or upsetting the Cassidys.

Both sides of Ashley had merit, but this was the one he'd once loved.

Hell, he was pretty sure part of him always would.

CHAPTER SIX

"Everything go a'ight at the Cassidy's today?" Nana stood at the sink, hand-washing the supper dishes when they had a perfectly good dishwasher she could use. One Ashley had bought her with one of her first paychecks when she'd gotten the job at the hospital.

After Nana's wrist had healed, Ashley had realized it was a losing battle. She couldn't convince her grandmother to use the automatic machine on a regular basis.

The woman was old school and stubborn. Just like Miss Eleanor. Which was exactly why Ashley had no business kissing Brody in the kitchen today with his grandmother just down the hallway. And why she shouldn't even consider meeting him later tonight.

So why was her pulse racing just thinking about the possibility?

"Yeah." Ashley answered her grandmother's question and then hesitated before adding. "Brody's home."

Nana flipped off the water and turned to face her. While grabbing a dishtowel to dry her hands, she said, "About time. It's been too long since that boy visited his folks."

"And far too long since I've seen you. Hey, Nana."

Ashley's eyes flew wide at the sound of his voice behind her. She spun to see Brody in the kitchen doorway.

"Brody Cole Cassidy, I know that your momma taught you to knock."

He grinned wide at Nana's censure as he strode across the kitchen. "Yes, ma'am, but Uncle Sam taught me even better how to sneak up on people and that's so much more fun."

Brody wrapped his arms around Nana. He lifted her until her feet no longer touched the ground, proof Uncle Sam had also given him some pretty strong muscles, as well, since Nana wasn't a small woman.

She slapped at his arms. "Put me down, boy."

Still smiling, he did as she asked, but he didn't take his hands off her waist. "Yes, ma'am."

Even as she was scolding him, Nana hadn't been able to completely hide the twitch of her own smile.

"Did you eat supper?" she asked.

"Yes, but I might as well not have since it wasn't your fine cooking." He dropped his hold on her and moved to the pot still on the stove. He sniffed the air and even before he lifted the lid, he glanced at

Nana and asked, "Chicken and dumplings?"

"It sure enough is. I see your nose is just as sharp as always." Nana was already reaching for one of the plates she'd just washed. "Sit yourself down. I'll serve you."

"Thank you." He looked like the teenage version of himself as he pulled out a chair and sat opposite Ashley at the table. "Hey, Ash."

That was it? He'd kissed the hell out of her in his family's kitchen, and then had followed her, uninvited, to her home, and all she got was a *hey*?

Of course, there was a good possibility he really was here for her grandmother—and the chicken and dumplings. Ashley knew Brody had truly loved both things—Nana and her cooking—while growing up.

Nana slid an overloaded plate of food in front of Brody.

As he tucked into it, Ashley wasn't sure if she should be insulted or relieved that he'd apparently come there tonight for Nana's food and not to see her.

"So, Ashley, got any plans for tonight?" The heat in Brody's eyes as he asked the question between forkfuls clued her into the fact that Brody's visit might have multiple purposes.

"Plans? Nope. Some of us have to work in the morning, you know." She could tease him just as well as he could tease her.

"Aw, come on. How much work could taking care of one eighty year old lady be?" His lips quirked with a smile as Nana let out a snort.

She faced the sink where she'd begun to scrub

the now empty chicken pot. "Lord, you know the answer to that, child."

"Ashley can handle it, Nana. I'm sure of it. She's very capable."

"Being capable ain't the problem and you know it."

"Now, Nana. You keep talking like that and I'm going to begin to think you're insinuating Miss Eleanor can be difficult." Brody smiled.

"Pfft. Ain't nothing I haven't told her myself and you know it."

Ashley grinned at the truth of it. Nana and Miss Eleanor always had a strange relationship. Nana was respectful but she'd never pulled any punches, and Miss Eleanor seemed to respect her more for it.

If Ashley had half the guts her grandmother had, things might have worked out very differently. She would have let Brody tell his family they were dating. She would have taken on the world of being a student and a wife without fear.

She glanced at Brody as he shoveled another forkful into his mouth, silently because how could he talk when he was eating so fast? He and Chris had always eaten like the hounds were about to steal their food if they didn't get to it first.

He was so familiar, yet at the same time, almost a stranger at this point.

What would have happened if she'd made a different decision back then? What was stopping her from making a different decision now?

It was crazy. He'd asked her to meet him, which must mean he was single.

She knew him enough to know what that would

mean if she did meet him. They'd be tangled up and naked before the dew settled on them.

Then what?

She knew the answer to that. He would go back to Virginia on Sunday and she would stay here and continue to work, because nothing had changed in that regard. His life, his future, was still the military and hers was still nursing.

"How's your brother been?" Nana asked, dishtowel in her hand.

"He's good. He's got himself a girlfriend. They seem pretty serious too. I think this might be it for him." Brody's eyes were bright as he passed along that information about his brother. Probably because he knew how shocked they'd all be at the news.

Chris—who'd reached the age of forty still a bachelor—had a girlfriend.

"About time. I never thought that boy would settle down." Nana echoed Ashley's thoughts aloud.

Brody let out a huff. "You and me both."

"And what about you?" Nana asked.

"What about me?" Brody leaned back from the table and pressed a hand to his stomach as if he was stuffed.

Meanwhile, all Ashley could notice was how his T-shirt clung to the torso defined beneath the tight cotton. She could see every ridge and bulge of his muscles.

There wasn't an ounce of fat on him but more than that, she could see the boy she'd known had definitely filled out and become a man.

"You got a girl?" Nana's question brought

Ashley's attention up from her perusal of the changes in Brody's body and on to the topic of if that body belonged to another woman.

His eyes connected with Ashley's as he said, "Nope."

"Why not?"

He turned to Nana to answer that question. "Who'd want me?"

Nana tipped her head to the side. "Eh, I bet I could find a girl or two who might."

"Well, please not on this visit. My dance card's full this week." He turned a meaningful glance toward Ashley before pushing his chair back from the table. Brody stood and turned toward Nana. "I'm saving all my time for my favorite girls. You. Grandmother. Mother. And Ash. Ain't got no time for anyone else besides the most important women in my life on this trip."

Nana dismissed his flattery with a mock scowl. "Uncle Sam train you how to lie too?"

"As a matter of fact, he did. Thank you for dinner." Brody grinned and pressed a kiss to Nana's cheek. He glanced at Ashley and said, "See ya."

Before he turned to leave the way he'd come his gaze told Ashley he'd still like to see her sooner rather than later. Tonight. At their place where they used to meet.

After the door closed behind him, Nana let out a breath. "That boy's still a whole mess of trouble. Time hasn't changed that any."

"No, it hasn't." Ashley had to agree.

Getting involved with Brody again would bring her nothing but trouble.

Even so, in the back of her mind she was running through a plan of how and when she'd slip out to meet him.

CHAPTER SEVEN

Dressed in PT clothes, Brody leaned into the doorway of the room where his mother and father were watching television. "I'm going out for a run."

His father glanced up. "Now? It's nearly nine o'clock."

"I'm used to keeping strange hours. Besides, it's still too hot to run in the daytime."

His mother stood and moved toward him. She stood on tiptoe and kissed him on the cheek. "I'll say goodnight then. Your father and I will likely be asleep by the time you get back."

"Okay. Goodnight. See you two in the morning."

There were many hours before then, and Brody had great hopes for that time . . . if Ashley came through and met him at their place.

He headed out the front door and ran on the road until he was out of sight of the house. Slowing his pace, he cut through a patch of trees and emerged along the edge of the town park.

It had been years since he'd been there with Ashley, but his heart pounded at memories that were as fresh as if he'd lived it all yesterday.

If things hadn't changed, she should be there any moment. Nana was a creature of habit. She'd watch television until nine and then head to bed. That was when Ashley had always slipped out of the house to meet him.

Back then she'd taken her bike. Would she now? He smiled at the thought, though more likely she'd drive her car.

He leaned against a tree and settled in to wait. If she was coming it would be soon.

What if she didn't show? Well then, he should probably thank God for saving him from making a huge mistake because deep down he knew reigniting things with Ashley could be the stupidest thing he'd done in recent memory.

With a deep breath, he sat on one of the swings. He was a little big for the child-sized swing set but that didn't stop him. He'd resigned himself to wait and see how the night would play out and he didn't feel like sitting on the ground to do it.

Besides the swing seemed like a less absurd choice for an adult male than the teeter-totter and the merry-go-round, though not by much.

Brody's cell phone vibrated in the pocket of his shorts. He had to stand to wrestle it out. For a brief moment, when he didn't recognize the number, he thought it might be Ashley. But she wouldn't know his number since he'd never given it to her.

"Hello?"

"Bro. Are you stateside yet?" Chris's voice, not quite clear, came through the phone.

"I am and it's about damn time you called me. I've been back in the country for days. I left you all kinds of messages and a note on the counter at our place."

"Well, since I'm not in the country you'll have to forgive me. My cell doesn't work here so I jumped on Jon's sat phone."

Brody frowned at that little piece of news that Chris was working out of the country with GAPS. "I didn't realize your job was OCONUS. Where the hell you at?"

Chris hesitated before he said, "This isn't a secure line."

"Are you fucking kidding me?" Eyes wide at that, Brody had to wonder what the hell kind of job Jon had landed for the company.

"Look, relax. I'm not saying you don't have the clearance to hear where I am or that I don't trust you. I'm just saying this isn't a secure line." Chris drew in an audible breath. "Remember the op last year while Jon and Zane were still in, and y'all had to swoop in and save a certain pretty young school teacher from the bad guys?"

"Yup." Brody remembered it well.

It wasn't every day a senator's daughter got kidnapped along with a class of schoolgirls. Zane had practically lost his mind during that situation since he'd been getting very friendly with Missy before that.

"Well, we got the same target and the same location."

Brody gathered from Chris's hints that somehow GAPS must be in Nigeria working against Boko Haram, the organization responsible for the kidnappings.

"But not the same package being recovered, I hope."

Chris chuckled. "No. As far as I know Missy is safely back in D.C., as if Zane would ever let her put herself in that position again."

"Yeah, I didn't think so." Brody had seen what had been done to those girls. Missy and her fellow teacher were damn lucky the team had found them as soon as they did.

"Sorry I wasn't there when you got home. I owe you a beer when I get back to Virginia."

"Damn right you do, but actually I'm on leave in Alabama."

"Kiss ass. Now I'm gonna look like the bad son that I'm not there too."

"Yup." Brody grinned, knowing Chris was only half kidding since their grandmother had already commented on Chris's absence. "Don't worry. I'll tell Grandmother you're too busy fighting bad guys to come home for a visit."

"Great. Thanks. That should go over like a fart in church. She didn't like me being away when I was active. She sure as shit ain't gonna understand it now I'm retired."

"Oh well. Guess you're out of the will then."

"Dickhead."

Brody grinned. He'd missed his brother, though he didn't feel compelled to tell him that. As he was enjoying the banter, a sound caught his attention. If he wasn't mistaken it was bicycle tires on grass.

Holy shit, Ashley was here and—just like in his imaginings—she'd arrived just as she used to in the old days. If that wasn't a sign that nothing had changed between them, at least in the physical department, he didn't know what was.

"Bro, I gotta go."

"What do you mean you gotta go? You're in Alabama with our parents and eighty year old grandmother. What the hell do you have to do instead of talk to me?"

"It's like nine-thirty here, dude. All the old folks are probably in bed by now."

"You're with a girl," Chris guessed.

"Not yet but in about thirty seconds I will be so yeah, love ya, get home safe, but I'm outta here. Bye."

Chris was in the middle of a colorful cuss as Brody hit to disconnect the call.

Smiling, he shoved the cell in his pocket and watched Ashley bring the bike to a stop.

What a difference a day made. If someone had told him yesterday he'd be practically jogging to get to Ashley, he would have told them they were nuts, after he'd punched them. But that was exactly what was happening.

She was here, after dark, at their old rendezvous spot, and that could mean only one thing. He hoped beyond reason that her appearance here meant that she wanted to take a trip back to revisit their past together as much as he did.

He reached her in no time. She swung one long leg over the seat to stand on two feet and then leaned the bike against a tree.

"Hey." She looked shy as she raised her gaze to meet his.

"Hey, yourself." There was no stopping Brody as he strode forward to cover the very short distance left between them.

He rested his hands on her hips, resisting the urge to do more before deciding he didn't want to hold back. Backing Ashley up until she was up against the tree he covered her mouth with his.

His hands didn't stay on her waist as the kiss got intense. Before he knew it, the skirt of her sundress was hiked up around her waist and he was pretty sure it had been his doing.

He was slipping his hand beneath the fabric of her underwear when she pulled back and said his name.

Drawing in a deep breath he got himself under control. "Yeah?"

Wincing, she reached up to touch her head. "My hair's stuck on something."

She wasn't asking him to stop, just telling him she was stuck on the tree.

He let out a breath in relief and reached up. Running his hand over her head he found the broken off branch that had snagged her hair.

After untangling her, he smiled. "Better?"

"Yes."

"Good." His heart was pounding so hard he wouldn't be surprised if she felt it. That didn't stop him from picking right back up where he had left off.

If she wanted him to stop, she was going to have

to ask. If she did, he'd stop, but until then there was nothing that was going to prevent Brody from having her.

He moved his hand around and ran his thumb over her bottom lip. Her lips parted and he could swear she trembled beneath his touch.

They were both far from virgins, but damned if she wasn't shaking. Him too, but that was from need and—if he was being honest with himself— the emotions pummeling him inside.

Being with Ashley wasn't going to be easy. As much as he wanted this, and make no mistake he did want it, this was not some quick hook-up. There was too much history between them.

A man couldn't have a one-night stand with the woman who'd once been his world. Who'd loved him and then left him beaten and battered.

Maybe he should thank her.

It was his trying to get over her that had gotten him through BUD/S. It was the memory of her refusing to even touch the tiny little chip of a diamond promise ring he'd bought her as an engagement ring that had him running full on into any challenge thrown at him.

Nothing the Navy could have done to him could have hurt him as much as Ashley had.

The painful memories had him crashing his mouth against hers. Claiming her with a rough crushing kiss.

He'd take back what had once been his. He'd show her what she'd given up. He'd possess her body and soul and then—

Then what?

He'd go back to work and leave her here, just like he had before because he felt the same about his career as she did about hers. It wouldn't be fair for either of them to ask the other to give up what they'd worked so hard for.

Drawing in a deep breath, he broke the kiss and leaned his head against hers.

"What's wrong?" she asked.

"Are we crazy for doing this?"

"Yes." At Ashley's answer he started to pull away. She pulled him back. "I didn't say I wanted you to stop."

He let out a short laugh. He didn't want to stop either. They could both worry about how to deal with the ramifications of their decision later.

Ashley brought her hands to his face. "I'm sorry I hurt you."

"I'm sorry I asked you to give up your future for mine."

The apologies on both sides were ten years overdue but somehow still necessary.

He was quiet, listening to her breathe amid the sounds of the night around them.

When she lifted her mouth to his, he stopped fighting it—stopped thinking—and kissed her. They were already in too deep.

While stroking his tongue against hers, he reached down. He moved his hand under her dress and slipped his fingers beneath the elastic of her underwear.

Her sharp intake of breath told him she wasn't immune to his touch.

Good to see that hadn't changed, although

hopefully he'd honed a few of his skills over the years.

"We doing this?" he asked before he took things any further.

Even after all his previous bravado about forging ahead and taking her no matter what, this was Ashley. His childhood friend. His first love. His only love. He needed to know she wanted this.

"Don't you want to?" she asked, sounding concerned.

As if she had to ask. He was throbbing beneath the fabric of his shorts. There was no way she could miss that the way they were pressed together.

"Yeah. Do you?"

"Yes." Her soft response was all he needed to hear.

Moving the fingers already happily nestled in her feminine warmth, he stroked her until she was panting, her whole body shaking where he had her pressed between him and the tree.

When she was a boneless, trembling mass, he scooped her up and carried her to the picnic table sheltered from view of the road by the trees.

He laid her on top and ran his hands up her long legs until he reached her panties.

As he pulled the garment down her legs, her eyes widened. "Here?" she asked.

"Yup." He smiled. "I'm too old to be laying on the ground."

"But someone could see—"

"I'll hear them before they see us. I promise." He was well trained. No one was going to sneak up on him.

Admittedly, they'd never trained for this particular scenario, but he was still confident as he tossed her underwear onto the bench and then lowered his head and kissed the skin of her stomach.

He kissed up her body, pushing the dress up as he went until he reached her breasts beneath the barrier of her bra.

As much as he wanted to strip her bare and feast on every inch of her, he was very aware of where they were.

He made do with slipping one full globe from beneath the lacey fabric and tonguing her nipple until she squirmed beneath him.

She'd filled out a bit over the years. Being a boob man, he wasn't at all opposed to the changes in Ashley's body.

Time hadn't been as kind to the park as it had been to Ashley's lush figure. He realized that as he slid his hands beneath her and felt the rough wood of the picnic table scrape against his skin.

Had it always been so rough? As a kid he hadn't cared or worried about splinters. Now he wasn't about to subject Ashley to the torture.

He pulled her upright and, sitting on the bench, guided her so she straddled his lap.

The heat in her eyes as she reached between them and stroked him through his shorts had him reaching for what else he'd shoved in his pocket before leaving the house besides his cell phone.

The elastic band on his shorts came in handy as he slipped his length free without having to undress. He made quick work of covering himself with the condom. Then Ashley was sliding down over him, stealing his breath, surrounding him with warmth he could swear he hadn't felt in a decade in spite of his having been with countless women during those years they'd been apart.

He could barely move with her in his lap, but he didn't need to. Ashley set the pace, slowly at first, and then speeding until he was lost in the sensation.

If anyone had come upon them he wasn't sure he'd have noticed, in spite of his promise to her that he would.

She let out a groan and he was done.

Bearing down and holding on to her with everything he had he clutched her close, his face buried in both her breasts and the fabric of her dress in an effort to smother his cry.

He finally had to turn his head as he tried to catch his breath.

It had never been that intense. Making love to Ashley as an adult was worlds different than it had been when he'd been an inexperienced youth.

Then again, he was different too.

They both were. They'd both lived and seen so many things outside of this tiny town.

"I can't believe you actually snuck out to meet me. And on your bike too."

"That makes two of us who can't believe it. And I had to take the bike. Nana might have heard me start the car." She pulled back far enough that she could look down at him. "This whole thing is kind of crazy, huh?"

Two presumably mature responsible adults and they were sneaking around and acting like teenagers.

If anybody caught them . . .

"Yup." There was no arguing that point so he didn't. Instead he just pulled her tighter against him again.

He was too content to care all that much about getting caught. If that were to happen he'd use the sailor freshly home from deployment excuse.

The beauty of that plan was that it wasn't even a lie. He'd been away from home too long and estranged from Ashley for even longer.

He wouldn't let that happen again. Even if it was nothing more than friendship, he wouldn't let another decade pass without seeing or talking to her.

The idea that maybe they could be friends with benefits flitted through his mind and he wasn't sure he liked it. They'd been too much to each other to be lovers who felt nothing now.

Besides, how long would a girl like Ashley remain without a man in her life? Brody had probably been lucky to catch her between boyfriends on this trip home.

What were the chances of that happening again? She was too smart and funny and beautiful to stay single long.

"Why aren't you dating anyone?" He couldn't stop the question from leaving his mouth.

After looking like she was surprised, she lifted one shoulder "I had such strange hours when I was working at the hospital. And here I don't see anyone except your family. I guess I work too much. Why aren't you dating anyone?"

"Same reason—work." Maybe they were perfect for each other after all. "You ever think about me? You know, over the years."

Brody realized his question was overly sentimental. He should have known being with her would raise the ghost of old feelings.

"Yes." She swallowed hard. "You ever think of me?"

"Yup." There was no denying that but he wasn't about to tell her the specifics about when the memories of her haunted him.

"So what now?" she asked.

He raised his gaze and found her watching him, waiting for an answer he didn't have.

"Now, this." Reaching up, he palmed the back of her head and brought her mouth down to meet his.

For the immediate future he intended to have her again. After that . . . he'd have to think about it.

CHAPTER EIGHT

Morning dawned as usual, as if nothing earth shattering had happened, but Ashley knew better. After last night with Brody, everything had changed, or maybe nothing had changed at all.

Her spinning thoughts and emotions made her almost dizzy as she moved through her early morning routine trying to pretend in front of Nana this was just another day.

In reality, her heart pounded and her mouth was dry thinking about arriving at the Cassidy's house this morning and having to face Brody.

Luckily, Nana had been so busy baking something special for her to bring to the Cassidy's for Brody, she hadn't been all that observant about how nervous and distracted Ashley was this morning.

Ashley kissed Nana goodbye, grabbed the basket filled with fresh muffins still warm from the oven, and headed for her car.

The drive to the Cassidy's wasn't too far. They lived on the other side of town but traffic wasn't an issue in this small town.

She reached the house without incident and was faced with Brody's truck in the driveway, physical evidence that he was still here when a small part of her had begun to doubt he would be.

The events of the past twenty-four hours seemed so surreal she half expected to wake at any moment and discover it had all been a dream.

But no, the door of the house swinging open and a smiling Brody standing in the doorway proved that if it was a dream, she hadn't woken from it yet.

"Hey." He pulled her toward him when she was close enough and planted a kiss on her mouth.

As much as she enjoyed the feel of his lips against hers, this was not the place or the time. "Brody, someone might see."

"So what if they do? Besides, my parents both left for work and Grandmother is in her bed complaining while drinking her coffee."

"Complaining she's hungry?" Ashley guessed with a smile as she moved into the hallway.

He closed the door behind her. "Yup. I was just about to see what I could do about that, as frightening as the thought of me cooking is. I sure do miss Nana, I can tell you that."

"Lucky for you, you always were Nana's favorite. She sent these." Ashley held out the basket to him and laughed when Brody's eyes widened as he took it from her.

"Muffins?"

"Yes, sir."

He groaned and even though it was obviously in anticipation of his favorite breakfast, the sound cut straight through her. It made her crave him again in spite of the fact they'd been together not even twelve hours before.

"Do I hear Ashley?" The old woman's voice traveled down the hall, strong in spite of her age and the distance.

"Yes, Miss Eleanor."

"Are you making breakfast?"

Brody lifted a brow. "I hope you get paid well for this job."

She laughed. Not nearly well enough but she kept that to herself. Instead she moved toward the bedroom doorway. "Nana sent a fresh batch of her muffins. Do you want one of those or do you want me to cook you something else?"

Miss Eleanor's eyes lit up as her gaze landed on what was in Brody's hand when he joined Ashley in the doorway.

"They're still warm." He held up the basket temptingly.

"Of course, I want one. Don't be silly. But I'll need a fresh cup of coffee to go with it."

"Yes, ma'am." Ashley turned to go get it for her when Brody's gaze caught hers for the briefest second before she broke the connection and headed into the hall.

The electricity shooting between Ashley and Brody should have been obvious to anyone watching, including Miss Eleanor. Good thing Nana's muffins were such a distraction.

She'd just reached the kitchen when she felt Brody come up behind her. "You could have stayed with Miss Eleanor. I can bring in the coffee," she said.

"If I had, I couldn't do this." He slid his arms around her from behind and nuzzled her neck.

She tipped her head to pull away, but all that did was give him better access to the over sensitive skin. "You shouldn't be doing that."

"So you keep saying. Sorry. I don't agree." The heat of his breath against her throat sent a tremor down her spine.

"Brody—" Ashley didn't have to finish her censure.

He pulled back and said, "Fine. Bring her the coffee, leave her with a pile of muffins to keep her busy, and then make an excuse to leave her for a little while."

Ashley frowned. "Why?"

"We have to talk."

Those four words seemed overly ripe with meaning but she nodded. "Okay."

It was all she could do to prepare Miss Eleanor's coffee with the impending conversation hanging over her like a shadow.

She managed it, even managed to deliver it without mishap, before she went back out to find Brody waiting for her in the hallway.

"All right. We have a few minutes."

"Gonna need more than a few." He yanked her into his bedroom just down the hallway.

"What are you doing?"

"Making up for lost time." Pulling her to him, he

lowered his head.

Ashley leaned back. "You said we had to talk."

"I lied." He tried to catch her mouth with his, but she managed to avoid him.

"No, you didn't. I can tell when you're lying and you meant it."

"Can you really?" He looked genuinely surprised.

"Yes. You have a tell. You can't look me in the eye when you lie."

"I already told you and Nana. I'm a highly trained operative. We're trained to lie." He grinned as if he was teasing but the truth was, he wasn't.

Ashley knew that because in a weak moment years ago, after she'd heard from Nana that Brody was training for the SEALs, she'd read anything and everything she could get her hands on about the subject.

"You might be trained to deceive strangers, but not family."

He let out a breath. "A'ight. You're right. We do need to talk. But after this. Okay?"

The *this* he spoke of was obvious as his palms pressed and held her tightly to his arousal while his thumbs traced circles against her hipbones.

"We can't have sex here and now." She had kept her voice low but hoped the intensity of her words got through to him.

"Just hush up and kiss me." His mouth over hers prevented further protest.

As her body warred with her mind, she decided she'd let him kiss her, but that was all. Nothing more.

The feel of the rock-hard muscles of his arms encasing her, making her feel safe and held, was enough to have her second-guessing that decision. As was the memory of the night before in the park.

She was about to abandon all reason when she finally pulled back from the lure of his kiss. "Seriously, Brody. She's right down the hall."

He grinned like a mischievous schoolboy. "Is that a challenge for me to prove how quiet I can be? You know, stealth is one of my finest traits."

Brody had many fine traits, in Ashley's opinion, but she couldn't let herself be swayed by any of them and give in to him now. Not while in his family's house with his grandmother just steps away.

Ashley changed the subject. "So what did you want to talk about?"

He dropped his chin, as well as his hands. "I got called in."

"You have to go back? Now?"

"Not immediately, but command wants me back sooner than planned."

"When?"

"I'm leaving first thing tomorrow morning."

"Oh." Amid the sick feelings ricocheting through her insides, Ashley couldn't help feeling grateful they'd have one more night.

But what was one night when she wouldn't see him again for who knew how long?

"Ash." He used his childhood nickname for her as he raised his hand to her face and stroked her cheek.

"Yeah?"

He shook his head. "I don't know what to say. I never planned this. Hell, I hadn't expected to find you here at all but I really didn't think we'd—"

"I know. Me either." They'd fallen back into each other like they were kids again. At least that's how it was for her. Judging by the regret she saw on Brody's face, he wasn't happy with this turn of events either. She said, "You don't have to worry. I know what this is."

He let out a short laugh. "Do you? Because I sure as hell don't know what this is between us. I don't want it to end but there's no way it can continue with you here and me—I can be anywhere and everywhere on an hour's notice."

"I know."

"I can't ask you to wait around for me. Just like I can't guarantee when I'll be back . . . or if."

She drew her brows down. "Don't say if."

Of course, she knew it was true. He could be hurt or killed, but that didn't mean she wanted to think about it, or talk about it.

"It's my reality, Ash." He let out a breath. "You were right back then to not want to buy into the life I live. It's too hard on relationships."

Hearing him admit that was like a final nail in the coffin of their relationship. It extinguished the last flicker of hope she'd managed to reignite.

"So . . . what do we do?" she asked.

"I know what I'd like to do."

"What's that?"

His hazel eyes met her gaze. "Make the most of the time we have left."

She had a feeling he'd say that. Typical Brody.

He'd been like that as a kid too. Live for the moment and don't worry about tomorrow.

He stood at arm's length, watching, waiting, she guessed for her to agree or not.

What would her saying no do? Only deprive her of grasping a few more moments with him. Deny her a chance to make more memories to hold on to for the next ten years.

It was sad but true that she'd take one more night with him over nothing at all.

"Okay." She glanced up to find him watching her.

"Are you okay? *Really* okay?" he asked.

She pressed her lips together and shook her head. "No."

He'd drive away and she wouldn't see him again for months, if not longer. He was eleven hours away by car and that was when he was in Virginia. Forget about all the times he wasn't even in this country.

Hooking his arm around her neck, he drew her to him and kissed her forehead. "Yeah, I know. Me either. We'll figure something out, okay?"

"Okay." It was easy to agree when he was here, holding her.

But once he left, once he went back to his life in the military and she back to the daily grind of her own job here, they'd both see more clearly. All the obstacles were still there. Were still insurmountable.

Even if she did look for a nursing job on the East Coast to be near him, the reality was he was away more than he was there. At least that's what she'd gathered from what Nana and his own family said.

Even if Miss Eleanor and her opinions about

Brody dating the help didn't scare Ashley as much now as ten years ago, the rest still stood. The distance. His responsibilities to the country he served.

How could she deal with that? Being alone in a new town with no family, no friends and no Brody half the time because his life belonged to the Navy.

Not just the Navy. His time was dictated by the mysterious command of whatever special unit he'd joined. The same people who'd given him a week off and then had taken it back just a day later.

She'd never come first in his life. At least not as long as he remained in this job.

Ten years later and nothing had changed. She was still in love with Brody Cassidy and their relationship was still impossible.

Ten hours later, Ashley was home with Nana.

Even as the anticipation built, she was still second-guessing her decision to meet Brody for one last time that night.

The buzzing of her cell phone on the living room table had her jumping. Trying to not look too anxious and arouse Nana's suspicion, Ashley casually reached for it and glanced at the display.

She frowned as she read the text from Brody.

Don't come to the park.

He'd insisted on programming their numbers and email addresses into both of their phones today while she tended to Miss Eleanor.

His attempt to make the distance not seem so great once they were separated, she supposed.

But they weren't separated yet and, even with the

overwhelming sadness that he was leaving again so soon, she'd really been looking forward to their last few hours together tonight.

After a glance at Nana to see if she noticed, Ashley confirmed her grandmother was too busy trying to guess the game show puzzle on the screen to worry about Ashley texting.

That still left the worry about why Brody didn't want to meet. With a feeling of dread, she punched in a question as her reply.

Why not?

I'm coming to you.

Brody's reply had her eyes widening. Ashley's fingers flew over the keys of the cell as she responded.

Nana is here!

Nana sleeps like a rock. Leave your bedroom window open. Be in bed by 10 PM.

She hesitated but in the end the idea of being with Brody in an actual bed rather than the park won out. Besides, Nana's room was on the first floor and at the opposite end of the house. That realization raised one concern.

You do know my room is upstairs?

He responded with a smiley face and two words, *No worries.*

A smiley face. From big bad Navy SEAL Brody who, unless he came armed with a ladder, was apparently planning to scale the walls of her home.

Yup. This whole situation was making them crazy.

Even so her heart was pounding with anticipation.

CHAPTER NINE

Brody was getting dressed to go out for a run—
or rather to *pretend* he was going out for a run while
he was actually going to Ashley's house—when his
cell phone vibrated in his pocket.

Pulling it out, he saw the same number as last
night and shook his head. Hitting to accept the call,
he said, "Bro, not that I don't want to talk to you,
but why do you insist on calling me at night?"

"Is there a problem?" Chris asked. "Am I
interrupting a big date?"

"Nope. Not yet anyway." He purposely made it
sound like a joke. The last thing Brody wanted to do
was talk about women with his brother over the
phone long distance. Over a beer when they were
both home, yeah, maybe then. But not now. He
changed the subject. "So how are things going
there?"

"Moving along slowly. Very slowly." Chris

sighed.

"Any ETA when you'll be home?" Brody asked.

"Nope. Even Jon and Zane aren't sure how long we'll be here yet."

If Brody got sent out immediately after getting back to Virginia, he wouldn't get to see Chris before he left. "Hmm, then there's a chance we'll miss each other. Our mutual *uncle* called and he needs me to travel again."

"What the hell? You just got home from deployment." Chris had understood Brody's hint that it was Uncle Sam who had recalled him. A man had to get creative when not on a secure line.

"I know but you know how it is."

"Yeah, I do. Damn, I was hoping you'd be around to keep an eye on Darci for me while I'm gone."

Brody's brows shot up. "Um, taking care of your girlfriend isn't exactly in my job description."

"I didn't mean take care of her. Just be there if she needs something. Rick's away right now too and I don't like her being in that house all alone."

"Then maybe she should have Ali stay with her. With Jon gone, Ali's on her own too."

"Yeah, I know. I suggested it but you know how Darci is."

"You mean obstinate and stubborn?"

"Hey. Watch it." The warning was evident in Chris's tone.

Brody laughed. "You've said as much yourself. Anyway, I'd love to help you and your girl, but I can't even stay here in Alabama as long as I'd planned."

"Shit. If they're yanking you off leave something big must be up." Chris voiced Brody's own suspicions.

"That's exactly what I'm thinking."

"A'ight. Well, keep me informed."

"I will if I can." In all likelihood Brody wouldn't know where he was going or when until the very last moment, and then he probably wouldn't be able to tell Chris anyway.

"So, how's the family?" Chris asked.

Brody jumped on the opportunity to tease his brother. "Dude, they're really pissed at you that you're not here."

"Fuck you. They are not."

Brody laughed. "Okay, only Grandmother is pissed. Says you're out of the will for sure."

"Yeah, well, if our family had Zane's kinda money I'd be worried you might be telling the truth. As it stands, not so much." There was the mumble of voices over the line before Chris said, "Shit, I gotta go. Give everyone there my best. Okay?"

"Will do. And Chris . . . stay safe. Okay, bro?" Brody didn't know exactly what Chris was in Nigeria doing but he knew no foreign travel came without risk. A GAPS job that required both of the bosses and Chris travel to the heart of Boko Haram country would be no exception.

His brother let out a snort. "Me? How about you? Take care of yourself, little brother."

"I will. Bye."

"Bye."

The line went dead and Brody lowered the phone from his ear.

He'd just gotten a very real reminder of what it was like to be the one left behind while a loved one was away.

It wasn't easy. He knew that, he'd just forgotten on some level.

Brody had been the one left home when he'd been just a kid still in school and Chris, just a little over ten years older, had enlisted. But Brody hadn't had the experience in awhile now that Chris had been retired from the teams for a few years.

Retired on not, Chris was currently back in harm's way leaving Brody home and concerned about his welfare.

Worrying sucked. Brody could only imagine the extent of the worry his family felt when he left, when he couldn't get in touch with them for weeks at a time.

And Ashley—she'd worry about him too now that they'd gotten close again. He knew it and it pained him to think about what it would do to her.

There was good reason SEALs rarely maintained a decent long-term relationship. And good reason why Brody didn't do serious relationships. It was too damn hard on everyone.

So why the hell was he planning on keeping in touch with Ashley now knowing how things would be once he left?

That was a good question, one that he had no answer to.

He opened his pack and pulled out a T-shirt so he could finish getting dressed to go see her, because apparently the reminder that this whole thing was pointless hadn't changed his mind about seeing her tonight.

CHAPTER TEN

The sound of scraping against the siding of the house just outside her window was so faint that if she hadn't been on edge waiting for Brody, Ashley might have missed it completely.

She threw the book she'd been trying and failing to read to the side and ran for the window just in time to see Brody clinging to the sash as his feet dangled below.

"Oh my God." She had tried to keep her voice low but the shock of seeing him hanging by his fingertips two stories in the air had stolen much of her control.

"Open the window and step back." Breathlessly, though not as much as she would expect considering, Brody issued that order.

She shoved the window, which had been cracked a few inches, all the way open and took a step back into the room.

Somehow he pulled and wiggled his massive body through the window opening, landing with not much more than a soft thud by her feet.

As she watched, wide-eyed and speechless, he grinned up at her from the floor. "Hey there."

"What are you doing? You could have fallen and killed yourself."

Pushing himself off the floor, he stood. As he brushed his hands together he glanced out the window and to the ground below. "From this height? Nah. It would take a much farther fall than that to kill me."

She didn't share his blasé attitude. "Why didn't you just sneak in the back door? Or even better, just meet me in the park like we'd planned?"

"Because this, darlin', is so much more fun." He stepped forward until his body was pressed to hers.

She felt the low rumble of his groan vibrate against her and she was lost.

It didn't matter that Nana was just downstairs. That Brody was leaving in the morning. That she didn't know when or if they'd ever be together again.

All those concerns took a backseat to the need his touch stoked inside her.

She ran her hands over his shirt and felt the muscles of his back, wishing she could feel the heat of this skin.

"You're overdressed."

His brows rose. "Am I? I could say the same about you."

"Then do something about it." Ashley didn't know where this vixen inside her had come from.

At the moment she didn't care.

As Brody pulled her oversized T-shirt up and over her head, it appeared he wasn't opposed to her new attitude either. He groaned again as he discovered she wasn't wearing a bra under the shirt.

He ran his hands over her bare skin as his gaze raked down her. "I missed you today."

She frowned at him, trying to hold on to her train of thought as he brushed her nipple with one thumb. "I only left your house a few hours ago."

"But I couldn't touch you like I wanted to at all during the day." He bent and pushed her shorts down her legs, leaving her bare.

"But we got to play Scrabble with Miss Eleanor." Ashley drew in a sharp breath as Brody ran his hands up between her legs.

"Please stop talking about my grandmother while I'm making love to you or we are in grave danger of me losing my abilities."

She reached between them to prove him wrong. "I'm not too worried. Everything feels fine to me in that department."

Brody's eyes narrowed as his gaze took her in. "I guess you're enough incentive to keep visions of Grandmother at bay."

He lowered his head to meet her lips with his, backing her up toward the bed as he did so. When her legs hit the edge of the mattress, her knees buckled and they both tumbled on top of the covers.

Groaning, he slid down the bed and positioned himself between her legs. "I've imagined all the things I could do with you in an actual bed."

Ashley had done the same, more times than

she'd like to admit. But all of her imaginings were never as good as the reality of having Brody there with her.

The heat of his mouth on her. Having his weight pressed against her. Of being encased in his strong, thick arms as he wrapped them around her.

Her imagination had missed all the good stuff that making love with Brody included.

The warmth of his breath against her skin. The soft sigh he let out as he slid inside her. The way he shook as he came.

Ashley tried to memorize it all. Every detail. It would be all she had once he'd left.

That one thought broke her resolve to not cry until after he'd left.

Unaware, Brody rolled his weight off her, but kept her held in his arms as he kissed her cheek.

He muttered a soft cuss and pulled back. "Are you crying?"

"No." She tried to keep the sound of her tears out of her voice but it didn't work very well.

He brushed his hand across her cheek, capturing a fresh drop of the moisture that spilled from her overflowing eyes. "Liar."

"Sorry."

Brody blew out a breath. "No. I'm the one who's sorry."

"Sorry that we did this?" she asked.

"No, that I'm making you sad. That I'm leaving you. Again."

They were both quiet for a moment. She didn't know what thoughts were running through Brody's head but in her own mind she was replaying the last time he'd left. The horrible scene the last time she'd seen him.

He had stood there in front of her then, looking thinner and tired but happy to be home for a short visit after finishing boot camp. He'd opened his soul to her by asking her to follow him. To be with him forever. Offering her the tiny band of gold with a small diamond in it he held between his fingers with a promise he'd buy her a better one when he could afford it.

When she said she couldn't do what he asked, she had seen the mingled hurt and anger in his eyes, at least what she could see through her tears.

"What did you do with the ring?" she asked.

"I carried it around with me for a while. Looked at it. Felt shitty. Finally I tossed it into the surf off Coronado." His laugh was short and humorless. "It was so small, so light, it barely reached the water even with me throwing it as hard as I could manage."

That image twisted her already pained heart. A shuttering sob escaped her.

"Come on, Ash. Don't cry."

"Why not?" This time tomorrow, Ashley would be alone in her bed and Brody would be gone again.

"Things won't be like before. I'll call you. And when I can't call, I'll email."

From somewhere far away and dangerous, she knew. They didn't talk about that though. Instead he held her for a long time, and she tried not to sniffle as a fresh wave of tears inevitably replaced whatever calm she'd managed to achieve after conquering the last bout.

Eventually, Brody kissed her forehead. "I should probably get going."

His announcement set off a panic inside her. "Will I see you in the morning?"

"No, I'm leaving before dawn to try and beat the traffic."

It was late. Dawn was only a handful of hours away. Even if he went directly to sleep when he got home, he'd be exhausted for the long drive tomorrow.

He stood and retrieved his clothing, piece by piece, from where he'd tossed it.

"Brody?"

"Yeah?" Brody bent to grab her T-shirt and handed it to her.

Ashley sat up and swung her legs over the edge of the mattress. "Do you really forgive me?"

"Yeah, I do. Because you were right. I didn't see it then but I do now. We were too young. I ended up being away more than I'm home. You had nursing school to finish." He lifted one shoulder in a half-hearted shrug.

After pulling the shirt over her head, she stood and moved closer to him. He grabbed and held both of her hands in his larger, warm ones. She let him, as grateful for the small contact as for the fact that he was still there. That he hadn't left her yet.

The tears streamed unchecked down her cheeks again.

Brody sighed and pulled her to him. "I know, Ash, I know. Saying goodbye sucks."

Yes, it did, but she didn't see him descending into a blubbering wreck like she was. Of course, she supposed big bad Navy SEALs didn't cry. Only the women they left behind did.

He pulled back and kissed her in spite of her streaming tears and runny nose. She was a mess and this was going to be his final memory of her, but he didn't seem to mind.

Lifting his hands, he cradled her face within his palms and deepened the kiss, thrusting his tongue against hers.

The kiss went on and on, but not nearly long enough. She leaned forward to prolong the contact as he pulled back and leaned his forehead against hers. "If I don't leave now, we're going to end up back in that bed. Then I'll never be able to bring myself to go."

That sounded like a good plan to her. Ashley swallowed away the sorrow. "Okay."

He drew in a breath and dropped his hold on her before turning toward the window to make his exit.

"Don't you want to use the door?"

Pushing the window wide, he glanced back and grinned. "Nah. Down's easier than up."

As sad as she was, his sneaking in and out of her second story bedroom by the window was so ridiculous she almost smiled.

He swung one leg over the sash and treated her to one last grin before he slipped out.

She stepped closer and was in time to see as he lowered himself by the strength of his arms alone, and then let go of the window sill and dropped straight down to the ground as she gasped.

He glanced up from where he'd landed on the lawn below, stood and offered up a wave before turning and taking off at a jog.

Obviously, he was fine from the fall. Ashley, on the other hand, might never recover from tonight, and watching Brody drop from the second story was the least of what would stick with her for a long time. Possibly forever.

She went to the bathroom to wash the tears from her face and brush her teeth before bed. She didn't anticipate getting any sleep tonight, not with the knowledge that Brody was just across town but would be gone by morning, but at least she'd be clean as she lay there not sleeping.

As she walked back through the door of her room she saw her phone light up on the nightstand. Diving for it, she saw Brody's name on the display and his text.

Don't be sad. Talk soon.

The tears started to flow anew.

With a sigh, she headed for the bathroom again and grabbed a wet washcloth to mop the salty tears from her cheeks.

It was going to be a long night.

CHAPTER ELEVEN

After battling traffic and one long ass drive he hadn't been in the mood to make, Brody made it back to base and to the meeting room just in time.

Rocky took one look at Brody's expression and asked, "What's up with you?"

Brody let out a derogatory snort at Rocky's question. "You mean besides that I left before sunrise and drove eleven hours from Alabama in the middle of what was supposed to be my weeklong leave?"

All for some bullshit meeting. About what, he didn't know. No one would say what it was about. Even the guys who hadn't been on leave didn't seem to know.

Thom busted through the door, the last of the team to arrive. He looked as unhappy to be there as Brody.

"What the fuck are they calling us in for? Anybody know?" Thom asked as he lowered himself into the empty chair next to Brody.

"Nope." Brody glanced at Thom, looking disheveled. He took a guess at why. "Girlfriend still in town?"

"Yeah." Thom blew out a breath. "She's not gonna be happy if we get sent out."

Since he was there, Brody hoped they did have a mission. It would really suck to have cut short his time home for nothing.

And Ashley—her sobs had haunted him for a good part of the drive reminding him of exactly how unfair it had been for him to have started things back up with her knowing he would be leaving.

"All righty, boys. Let's get down to business." The team commander entering the room tore Brody's mind away from Alabama and back to business—whatever that might be.

Brody glanced up, about to wait for the answer to his unasked question, when a second man walking into the room behind the commander had his eyes widening.

"Some of you who've been around for a bit might recognize this man . . . " As the team commander finished the introduction, Grant Milton stood shoulder to shoulder with him. "He's been brought in because of his first hand knowledge and experience with our target and the area. I'm going to let him take over."

Apparently Grant's request to move back from his training assignment had been approved. At least for this assignment.

Whatever this mission was, they were about to find out as Grant stepped forward.

"Boko Haram." Grant's gaze hit on Brody and Thom. "Those of you who were with me on this team last year are intimately familiar with this enemy and with the men currently in N'Djamena working to stop them.

"The Multi National Joint Task Force and the member countries of the Lake Chad Basin Commission have met to organize a joint force to fight Boko Haram. A private military company staffed by former DEVGRU operatives has been brought in to advise on and implement the plan, including helping to train the forces."

From what he knew from Chris, and that Grant had looked directly at him when speaking, it wasn't too much of a stretch for Brody to guess that the PMC mentioned was GAPS and the men currently in Africa training others and brainstorming some sort of battle plan were Chris, Jon and Zane.

Grant continued, "In addition to the kidnappings, and the suicide bombings that continue to kill hundreds of locals, we have proof that Boko Haram has sworn allegiance to ISIS."

Rocky mumbled a cuss beneath his breath that echoed pretty much what Brody was thinking. Separately the two terrorist organizations were bad enough. Allied, they'd be worse.

"The joint forces will be deployed to two command posts. One in Nigeria. One in Cameroon. The timetable is to eradicate Boko Haram from the region within three months."

Brody had to smother his reaction to that ridiculously unrealistic timetable as he wondered which politician came up with it.

He had to wonder one more thing. What did this have to do with his unit?

When Grant drew in a big breath to continue, Brody had a bad feeling he knew and that for the next three months he wouldn't be enjoying any of those American amenities he'd missed while in Turkey over the past six months.

And then there was Ashley . . .

They'd just found each other again and now they'd be on two different continents. She wasn't going to be happy about that. He wasn't thrilled about it himself, but he was used to this life. She wasn't.

"I'm sure you're all wondering what our role in this plan is. POTUS has not authorized boots on the ground. We'll be going in strictly in an advisory capacity. We are to intervene only when and if there is imminent danger to the U.S. citizens in the region."

Advisory capacity, his ass. Brody rolled his eyes at the political bullshit. Where they were going, where GAPS currently was, danger was imminent every second of every day. But they all had to spew the same official rhetoric to keep the public and the politicians happy.

Meanwhile, Brody would definitely enjoy reminding Chris often that his SEAL team had been brought in to play babysitter to GAPS.

That was one bright side to this whole assignment.

Decimating Boko Haram would be another—if that could be accomplished. Brody had his doubts about that, especially about it happening within the allotted three-month window, but after having seen the damage done to the people by the fanatical organization, he was sure hoping for another crack at them.

The team commander stepped forward again to take over the floor from Grant. "Pack your gear, go home and kiss your loved ones goodbye. We go wheels up at zero-six-hundred."

Thom mustered a curse. "We just got back."

Brody shot Thom a glance and saw his unhappy expression. "Yup. Better go make nice with the girlfriend."

"Ginny is not going to be happy." Thom sighed.

Rocky leaned forward. Single and unattached with no worries in this regard, Rocky didn't look all that sympathetic to Thom's situation. "This is your life. She better get used to it if she's gonna be a part of it."

Thom let out a snort. "Tell her that."

Any other day, Brody would have been completely on Rocky's side in this. Any SEAL stupid enough to try to have a relationship while active duty got what they deserved. But today, Brody was faced with having to call Ashley and explain he was leaving the country again, without telling her why and to where.

He didn't want to make that call, mainly because he didn't want to hear the tears in her voice.

This relationship shit was so far out of his comfort zone, the thought of calling Ashley had his pulse speeding faster than the announcement of the team deploying to Nigeria to fight Boko Haram had.

How crazy was that?

Brody didn't like the feeling. It was a distraction he couldn't afford right now. Not when he had orders to get ready to leave in twelve hours.

Pushing his chair back from the table, Brody stood and glanced down at Rocky. "I'm going to pack my gear. You coming?"

Rocky stood. "Yup. I'm right behind you. Packing up should be easy, at least, since I never completely unpacked all my shit from last time."

"True that." Brody turned for the hallway, Rocky right behind him as they headed out the door, as promised.

This—getting ready to deploy, having the team he trusted above all else at his back—this was familiar territory.

It felt good to be doing something he did well.

He'd deal with telling Ashley later.

CHAPTER TWELVE

"Ashley!"

The sound of her name being bellowed from the bedroom had Ashley clenching her jaw.

For a supposedly ailing woman, Miss Eleanor could sure yell plenty loud. Ashley usually had patience for the old woman, as she did with anyone under her care, but after getting next to no sleep she was running a little short.

Today, she didn't have it in her to paste on a smile and pretend everything was all right. That getting Miss Eleanor another glass of sweet tea was the biggest pleasure in her life at the moment. Or that she found the show on TV as fascinating as the old woman did.

All that on top of her other duties such as changing the bed sheets, bathing her, helping her to the toilet, and dealing with the consequences when she didn't quite make it.

Arriving at the Cassidy house this morning and finding the driveway empty of Brody's truck made the emptiness Ashley felt at his absence increase tenfold.

Now, nearly at the end of her shift, she still didn't feel much better about things, just more tired.

Sighing, she made her way to the bedroom. "Yes, Miss Eleanor?"

"Can you bring me one of your grandmother's muffins? Brody says there's some leftover in the fridge. It will be cold, so you'd better warm it up for me first."

Was the old woman confused or just remembering now something Brody had told her before he'd left?

Drawing in a breath for strength, Ashley said, "I'll look again, but I don't remember seeing any. Maybe they're all gone now. When did he tell you this? Yesterday?"

"No, he told me just now when he called to check on me." She held up the phone as Ashley felt the blood drain from her face.

"Oh. Okay. I'll go see." She made a beeline for the hallway and pulled her cell out of her pocket.

There were no missed calls or texts and she had good signal as evidenced by the fully lit up bars on the display.

Carrying the phone in her hand all the way to the kitchen so she could keep an eye on it, she watched and waited. She only took her gaze off the device so she could look inside the fridge for these muffins Brody had found important enough to call his grandmother about when he hadn't bothered to even text Ashley.

She tried to reason away her hurt and anger.

Brody shouldn't be texting while he was driving. It wasn't safe. And he probably didn't want to call her cell phone during the day because he'd known she was working. So really, it made sense he'd dialed his house number, maybe even on the chance that Ashley would answer.

Dammit. She'd heard the phone ring too but had ignored it because she'd been in the middle of something. Next time, she was grabbing it, no matter what.

Sighing, she finally remembered why she was standing in front of the open refrigerator door. The muffins.

Where were they? She didn't see them on any of the shelves. Bending over, she yanked open the vegetable drawer and there they were, in a plastic bag nearly hidden behind the lettuce.

Ashley shook her head. No doubt Brody had put them there. Probably, knowing him, so no one else would find and eat them. Now that he'd been called back, he was willing to share the bounty.

Typical Brody.

She couldn't help her sad smile at the thought as she reached for the bag. Taking one out, she glanced at the time displayed on the microwave before popping a muffin inside and setting it to warm for twenty-seconds.

It was getting late in the afternoon. He should be nearing the end of his drive shortly. She just had to be patient.

Soon the Cassidys would be arriving home from

work, one at a time, and Ashley would be relieved of duty. Then, when Brody knew she was home and could talk, he'd call.

Four hours later, Ashley was still waiting for that call.

She'd done the math. She'd done a web search. She'd calculated the distance and the time. He had to be back in Virginia by now.

If not, then something was very wrong. Like fiery-crash-on-the-highway kind of wrong.

She finally convinced herself it was her duty to call him and make sure he was okay. If Brody hadn't wanted her to call, he wouldn't have made sure his number was in her cell. Right?

Armed with that justification, she glanced over at Nana seated in her favorite chair with her eyes glued to the television.

"I'm going to head upstairs," Ashley said.

Nana frowned. "You a'ight? It's early."

"I know, but I'm kind of tired."

"Then it's sleep you need. Always listen to your body and you can't go wrong."

Listening to her body, and letting it convince her to go to bed with Brody, was exactly what had put Ashley into such a tizzy.

She kept that observation to herself. "Yes, ma'am. Goodnight."

"Night, baby girl."

It was all Ashley could do to keep herself from sprinting from the room and barreling up the stairs. Now that she had made the decision to call him, she couldn't get alone quickly enough.

Once in the privacy of her bedroom, she closed the door and pulled out the cell that had never left her side all day as she'd waited for some kind of contact from Brody.

She punched the screen to dial his number and, feeling breathless, listened to the ringing.

"Cassidy." His formal address took her aback.

"Brody, it's me." She thought better of not identifying herself and added, "Ashley."

"Sorry. I've got my earpiece in and the phone in my pocket so I didn't know who was calling." He blew out a breath sounding stressed or at least distracted from whatever he was so busy doing. "Anyway, what's up?"

His continued business-like tone and complete lack of warmth continued to confuse Ashley.

More, it was starting to make her stomach hurt as her insides twisted with regret. Regret that she'd called him. That she'd slept with him.

"I was worried about you on that long drive. When I didn't hear from you, I had to know that you'd made it safely."

He smothered a cuss. "I'm sorry, Ash. I got here just in time for my meeting and I've been running ever since trying to get things ready."

"Ready for what?" she asked.

A long stretch of silence was the only answer to her question until he finally said, "Um."

"You can't tell me where you're going or what you're doing." She pressed her lips together.

On some level she'd known what being with an active duty SEAL would be like, but that didn't make the reality of it any easier to deal with.

"Look, I'll get in touch with you when I can. Okay?"

So he could continue to avoid her questions and act like she was annoying him? No, thank you.

"That's fine, Brody. Don't bother. Maybe I'll see you around whenever you're home again." As she lowered the phone from her ear she heard him say her name.

With more willpower than she thought she possessed, or maybe motivated by plain old anger, she punched the display to disconnect the call.

She poked at the screen again a couple more time out of frustration and then tossed the phone onto her bed.

It was completely irrational and immature to take her bad mood out on a cell phone that would cost her plenty of money to replace should she manage to break it. Right now she didn't care.

Even so, when she heard the buzz of an incoming message, she dove for the cell.

We'll talk when you're feeling better.

She read his message, nostrils flaring as she breathed in fast and hard.

Feeling better? She wasn't sick. She was pissed off at him and for damn good reason.

What the hell? What kind of man could speak sweet words to her one day and then treat her like she was a telemarketer bothering him by calling his phone the next?

Mumbling to herself, Ashley stalked back and forth across the small space of her room like she was a caged animal.

When the raw mad gave way to angry tears and

then finally pure exhaustion, Ashley flopped onto the bed.

Wiping her eyes, she raised her cell and checked the display. Nothing. Still she kept the phone in her hand so she wouldn't miss a call or a text if Brody contacted her to apologize.

She truly was a pitiful mess.

CHAPTER THIRTEEN

"Everything okay?" The question came from Rocky, who again was proving too observant for Brody's liking. Especially now as Brody stood surrounded by his gear with the phone still in his hand.

Brody could have lied, but he wasn't in the mood. "Nope."

"Wanna talk about it?" Rocky asked.

"Nope." Brody would listen to his brothers in arms vent from sun up until sundown if they needed to, but he'd never had been one to spill his guts.

Yeah, he could bitch about command and regulations as well as the next guy, but when it came to the personal stuff? *That* he tended to keep to himself.

"Wanna get a drink?" As opposed to the previous inquiry, Rocky's follow-up question was a welcome one.

That suggestion, Brody could get on board with. "God, yes."

They were pushing out early in the morning if things remained the same, which most likely they wouldn't. There was always the chance they'd get called in before then.

Such was the nature of the military. Spec Ops even more so. But Brody had been playing this game for long enough he knew how much he could drink and still function.

He could definitely have a beer or two and still be ready to board a transport with all his shit in tow on an hour's notice if necessary. And he'd sleep on the transport so that wasn't an issue.

Hell, he could stay up all night. It might be better actually if he was tired enough to fall sleep on the trip naturally rather than take something to knock himself out. He could come up with all sorts of justification for himself that going out now was a good idea when it all boiled down to one thing— after that call with Ashley he needed a drink.

"We going to the strip club?" Rocky asked.

"I don't know. Maybe just the bar. That okay?" Brody glanced at Rocky in time to see the man's dark brows shoot high.

It seemed like all it took was a couple of days home with Ashley and Brody had lost his taste for strippers. He tried not to dig too deeply into why that was true.

After an odd and unnecessary pause, Rocky nodded. "Sure, Brody. No problem. Whatever you want. The bar it is."

Brody had to think that was a hell of a lot of

words out of Rocky when a simple *okay* would have worked, but he wasn't in the mood to press it. Instead he glanced in his pack one more time to be sure he'd stowed the last of what he needed before he shut it and shoved it onto the shelf.

Satisfied he'd be ready to go when the time came to move out, he locked the cage and turned toward Rocky. "Ready?"

"Yup. Let's go."

Grant was in the hallway as Rocky and Brody headed for the exit. He asked, "You two heading out?"

"Yup." Brody nodded.

"Heading to the bar." Rocky offered up their destination when Brody specifically had not.

Grant might not technically be the commander on this op but he was close enough Brody had thought it best to keep their plans to go out drinking hours before deploying to themselves.

Even though they had been out at the strip club with Grant just days ago, Brody shot his teammate a glare and tried to cover by saying, "Just to grab one last burger before we ship out."

Grant grinned. "Yeah, okay. See you back here tomorrow."

"Yes, sir." Rocky finally stepped it up and acted like Grant was an officer and not a drinking buddy, much to Brody's relief.

When they were outside and in the parking lot, Brody shot Rocky a glance. *"We're going to the bar?* You don't tell an officer shit like that."

Rocky rolled his eyes. "So what? It wasn't like I told him we're planning on doing shots until we pass out, which we're not. We're allowed to go wherever the hell we want. Jeez. Chill, dude."

Jaw clenched, Brody drew in a breath through his nose.

Rocky stopped dead in his tracks. When Brody kept walking, Rocky said, "Cassidy."

Brody stopped and turned back. "What?"

"I don't know what the fuck crawled up your ass during your leave that put you in this piss poor mood, but you'd better get over it before we hit the ground."

Brody didn't need to be told that, even if it was true. "I know. I'll be fine."

Rocky watched him for a beat, before nodding and taking the few steps to close the distance between them. "So you're really not gonna tell me what happened on your leave?"

Brody laughed, the tension broken by Rocky's ridiculous question. "No. I'm really not."

This was how it was between teammates. Guys could go from arguing, even nearly coming to blows, one moment and then be joking with one another the next.

Rocky shook his head. "Damn. You're no fun. I was stuck here in boring old Virginia Beach for the whole week we got to be stateside. Meanwhile you got to go to Alabama and you won't tell me shit. How am I supposed to live vicariously through you?"

Brody let out a snort. "Spoken like a Yankee who's never been to Alabama. Believe me. You're not missing anything."

"Yeah, yeah. So you say." Rocky shot him a

sideways glance. "I'll tell you all about the new stripper they hired at the club. Jasmine, and believe me she is as sweet as her name."

"Her fake name, I'm sure." Brody shook his head, smiling at Rocky's enthusiasm.

Rocky waved away the comment. "So what? Hell, like Rocky's my real name?"

"It's not?" Brody feigned shock. "You've been lying to me all this time? I feel so used."

Grinning, Rocky shook his head as he stopped next to the door of his truck. "Get in. I'll drive. You know, in case you're feeling a little tipsy after your *hamburger* and don't want to drive."

"Eh, it could happen." Brody bobbed his head and moved to the other side of Rocky's truck.

Brody wasn't worried about keeping his head in the game once they landed. He was feeling better already.

It would be even easier to remain on task once in Africa with the whole team, their singular focus the mission.

Among all of the things that made it possible to do this job, compartmentalizing was one of the most valuable.

It's what allowed him to move between normal life and military life with the flick of an internal switch. To act like a normal human one day and turn into an analytical trained warrior another.

Civilians didn't get it. Ashley for sure wouldn't understand it, but Brody had already stowed his emotions about her and their situation. Those feelings would remain locked away until it was convenient and safe for him to deal with it all.

Compartmentalizing was not just instinct. It was a necessary protocol, as much as locking up his kit between ops was.

It meant survival for not only him but for the entire team—but there was a price to pay. Men who could do what he did didn't make for great boyfriends or husbands or fathers, either, he supposed.

That thought was one more thing he'd have to put away to deal with later.

CHAPTER FOURTEEN

"We're here. Who called in the cavalry?" Brody made the general announcement to the men in the room, grinning as he did so.

His brother Chris turned, scowl firmly in place. "Pfft. Not fucking me. I didn't even find out they were sending the team here until yesterday."

Brody clutched his hand to his chest over his heart and gasped. "I'm hurt. Is that any way to treat your brother?"

Chris came forward and pulled Brody into a one-armed hug. "As your brother, I'm happy to see you. But that these assholes think GAPS needs reinforcements is more than a little insulting, if you ask me."

Jon Rudnick came up beside Chris and shook Brody's hand. "Good to see you, Brody. And don't listen to your brother. I'm happy to have the help. Especially since it's from guys I know are qualified and I trust. The more boots on the ground, the better."

"Shh. No one authorized boots on the ground, remember? The team's here as 'consultants'." Brody couldn't help his grin over that bullshit. Chris let out a snort at it too.

Brody looked around them. "Nice digs you got here."

"Eh, could be worse." Chris lifted one shoulder.

"True that." As far as training camps went, Brody had been in worse. They all had.

And he couldn't complain about the company. It would be great to kick some Boko Haram ass alongside Jon and Zane, like they had done when the two men had still been on the team.

That thought had Brody asking, "Where's Zane at?"

"He's on the sat phone again." Chris's eye roll had Brody wondering if civilian life had made Zane soft in the field.

"Girlfriend?" Brody asked.

"Worse. Senator Greenwood. The man recommended us for this job and he funded us back when his money meant life or death for our idea to open GAPS to begin with, so don't get me wrong, I'm grateful—"

"But," Chris interrupted Jon, "the good senator has been up our ass since we got here, wanting to know every move before we make it."

"So far Zane's been handling him fine so I'm gonna let him continue." Jon held up his hands, symbolically surrendering control of the senator to his partner in GAPS.

"Sounds like a good plan to me." Brody couldn't blame Jon one bit for his hands-off approach with Senator Greenwood.

Politics and bullshit were the things Brody didn't like about his job, but there was no getting away from them. Apparently not even after separating from the military as Jon and Zane had.

Besides, against all odds Zane, the former playboy, had been dating Missy Greenwood. They'd been serious and, amazingly enough, monogamous for a long while now.

Since it looked like Zane was only one gold band away from becoming the senator's son-in-law, the job of handling the man clearly belonged to him.

"So what do you and the senator have planned for us?" Brody grinned as his brother scowled at his question.

"We have a meeting set with your team and the command at sixteen-hundred." Jon glanced at the watch on his wrist.

Brody cocked a brow. "A'ight and what's the plan?"

He was in a room alone with his brother and one of his good friends with the door closed. He'd be damned if he waited until sixteen-hundred to hear the official company line about why they were here and what was going to happen.

His brother shot Jon a look before motioning for Brody to come closer.

"You flew into here. N'Djamena." Chris poked a finger at a spot on the map spread out on the large table dominating the space. "We're currently set up in the command post here. The target's stronghold is here, in the middle of the Sambisa Forest. The sheer density of that forest has been their best protection so far."

Jon stepped closer and pointed to a place not far from where Chris had indicated the target was. "There's a road running just to the south of the forest. Given the terrain, that would be the easiest way to approach the camp."

Brody considered the area and the scenario. "Which is why they'll likely be watching for anyone to approach from that direction."

"Yup. That's why we're going to have a decoy unit approach from that direction. Once the target has taken the bait and their attention is diverted by Alpha unit to the south, we'll drop Bravo and Charlie units into the forest by helo north of the camp." Chris tapped an area on the opposite side of the camp from the road.

Brody raised his gaze from the map to look at Jon. "We were in that forest. A unit patrolling in is not going to be quiet enough to avoid notice."

Especially if they were planning on using the newly trained local forces. Experienced DEVGRU operatives were silent and deadly, but Brody could easily imagine how much noise troops not trained to be covert could make while crashing through the forest.

"We plan on Bravo and Charlie fast-roping in. We've got the Marines periodically flying the CH-53s we'll be using over the area to get the target used to hearing helicopters overhead."

Brody snorted. "That's good, because there ain't no hiding one of those Super Stallions."

The massive helicopters Jon was talking about using to drop troops into the middle of the Sambisa Forest were nearly three stories high.

Jon continued, "While Bravo unit camps out at a far enough distance away to avoid detection by the target and waits, Charlie unit—Brody, that'll be you and your team—is going to move in close enough to observe the target. Now, besides just using the density of the forest for protection, Boko Haram has also set up mines and booby traps in the area."

"So my team will have to clear a path for Bravo unit."

"Yes." Jon nodded in response to Brody. "But that's not your only purpose. We have bigger plans for you than mine sweeping. We know from satellite images the target travels in and out of the forest fairly often by truck. Your goal will be to liberate one of those trucks for our use."

Brody laughed, since he'd liberated a truck or two during the mission to rescue Missy Greenwood from that same forest. "One of my favorite things to do."

Jon smiled. "Yes, I remember. Once we have possession of the vehicle, we'll move quickly into a three-pronged attack. Bravo unit will move in from the north, while at the same time Alpha unit will make their move from the south."

Chris continued where Jon left off, "And by then the camp will be so crazy, who's going to pay any attention to one of their own trucks driving in? That is, until Charlie unit pops out of the back and rains hellfire on them."

Brody nodded. "So we'd be driving a Trojan

Horse right into the middle of their camp."

"Yup." Chris looked very pleased with the plan, leading Brody to believe his brother had some hand in coming up with it.

Brody glanced from one man to another. "It's crazy enough, it might just work."

"That, my brother, was my thought exactly." Chris grinned.

CHAPTER FIFTEEN

The evening game show on television wasn't holding Ashley's attention. She couldn't muster the energy to care if the family guessed the most popular answer to the survey question or not. How could she care when she was creeping up on forty-eight hours with no contact from Brody?

Yes, she'd been angry when he'd said they'd talk after she'd calmed down, or felt better, or whatever his ridiculous words had been. But that was back when she believed they actually would talk again.

Now, a full two days later, she was beginning to wonder.

She drew in a deep breath and let it out louder than she intended.

"What's wrong, baby girl?"

"Nothing, Nana." Ashley didn't even have to look directly at her grandmother. In her peripheral vision Ashley saw the movement clearly as the woman's dark brows shot high.

"Child, I raised you from the moment you came out of your momma. Don't you think you can lie to me." The tone was one Nana had used on Ashley as a child.

That only made Ashley scowl and probably look like a child as she said, "I'm not lying. There's nothing wrong."

At least nothing that Nana could fix. Ashley had made her bed—and laid in it with Brody—and now she'd have to deal with the aftermath.

That she certainly couldn't tell her God-fearing, switch-raised, Southern Baptist grandmother.

With a huff, Nana hoisted her large frame forward and snatched the remote control from the coffee table. Ashley watched as she smashed the buttons with her thumb until there was no more sound on the television. Only silent moving pictures.

Ashley sighed, defeated. "I'm upset that Brody said he'd call and he hasn't."

"Girl, he's a little busy, don't you think?" Nana asked.

"But it's like his job is always more important than his family and his friends."

"Maybe it is."

"To him, maybe, in his own self-centered little world."

"It's more than just *to him*." With the remote still clutched in her hand, Nana tipped her chin toward the television while at the same time pushing the button on the remote to change the channel. When a news station showed on screen, she slowly raised the volume.

The announcer's voice rose until Ashley could hear it clearly as it accompanied horrifying images. Bodies of Syrian refugees—some of them young children—washing up on the public beaches in Turkey. People who had risked and lost their lives to flee the horrendous conditions in their own country.

The story ended and the images changed, switching to Nigeria. There the newly elected president was promising he'd work to defeat the Islamic militant organization who'd kidnapped all those schoolgirls over a year ago. He vowed to do so by the time he took office at the end of the month, a promise the expert interviewed next declared completely unrealistic.

The images switched one more time to a reporter in the United States speaking about an American arrested after a failed bomb attack. One he'd planned after pledging loyalty to ISIS on Facebook.

Throughout the news broadcast, which delivered all the horrors happening in the world into their living room with succinct rapid-fire precision, Ashley didn't know what to say.

Nana was silent as well, but it was clear she was waiting for Ashley to acknowledge the point—that Brody's job was important.

He was responsible to more people than just her and his family. He had to worry about life and death worldwide, not just that his old girlfriend—and current hook-up—was waiting for his call so she could cry some more over him leaving.

She drew in a breath. "Okay, Nana. I get it. You

can change the channel now."

"In a minute." Her eyes stayed glued to the screen as she shook her head and let out a small tsk-tsk sound over the last story about the homegrown terrorist.

Ashley didn't understand it either but she wasn't as surprised as Nana. After working in the hospital ER, Ashley had witnessed all sorts of crazy.

Nana didn't make a move for the remote control again through the next commercial break and Ashley feared she'd be subjected to cable news for the rest of the night.

Over the depressing news being reported, she'd take watching a silly game show any day.

Finally the coverage moved on to the current presidential election. One look at Donald Trump on the screen had Nana scowling and fumbling to change the channel.

Ashley smiled at the speed with which Nana had changed her mind about what they'd been watching. She knew if Obama had come on screen instead, they'd have been glued to the station for the duration.

She realized she did feel better. It hadn't been a soul bearing confession to Nana, but just talking about Brody with her grandmother had helped her reason away the anger.

Nana had lived a long hard life. She'd seen a lot of things. Overcome more than any woman should have to, from losing her husband young to having to raise Ashley when her flighty daughter had taken off and left her with her unplanned granddaughter. Through it all, she'd come out the other side.

If Ashley had the nerve to confess all that had happened with Brody, she was sure Nana would have a world of wisdom.

She weighed the ramifications versus the benefits of talking openly with her grandmother. Good girls didn't do what she'd done with Brody unless they were married. Not as teenagers and, adult or not, not even in their late twenties.

Surely Ashley was too old now for Nana to take a switch to her bare bottom, right?

Glancing at the woman, still big and strong at near eighty, Ashley decided she wasn't willing to test the theory and find out.

She'd reconcile herself to Brody's life and career on her own and when he called—God, how she hoped he called—she'd tell him she understood how important it was. Then, together, maybe they could figure out how to make it work.

Whatever *it* was. Maybe if she knew *that*—what they were to each other—she'd know how to deal with it.

They definitely should have spent more time talking and less time doing what they'd done.

Maybe she deserved that beating after all.

CHAPTER SIXTEEN

"Questions?" The team CO asked while glancing around the meeting room.

Rocky raised his hand. "So we're telling the joint forces' troops we're on a training exercise?"

"Yup." The CO glanced at Grant, who nodded in agreement.

"But in reality we're inserting into the forest just a couple of klicks from where we think the target's leaders are holed up?" Rocky followed up on his first question.

"That about covers it." Zane, standing next to Grant for this meeting, nodded.

Brody was happy to see Zane was finally off the phone with the senator so he could attend this meeting.

"That's nuts." Dawson, one of the newer guys on the team, shook his head.

Chris blew out a breath. "I'll tell you what's

nuts. It's that the Nigerians announced their last attempt against Boko Haram ten days in advance, which gave the target plenty of time to move their leaders out."

Rocky's eyes popped wide. "Holy shit. So when you gonna tell them the truth?"

"When we get where we're going. Maybe." Jon shrugged.

Next to Rocky, Thom shook his head. "It's bad enough we have to fight the bad guys. Now we have to deceive the good guys too."

"But are they going to believe what we tell them?" Rocky glanced back to Grant as he asked the question.

Grant answered, "Sure. Because we've convinced them we believe their theory that taking Boko Haram in the forest is too difficult. We're letting the local forces continue their operation to retake control of the towns previously lost, one at a time."

Jon nodded. "Boko Haram abandoned Gwoza and a couple of other small villages rather than fight, but the reality is until we defeat them they'll just move right back in again after the ground forces leave."

Zane took over explaining the situation. "The target's changed goals and tactics. It seems they've abandoned the hope of controlling the region and running their own state. They're being forced underground but they're not gone. They'll be using guerilla tactics. I think we can expect small, more frequent, targeted attacks. But not all of the attacks will be smaller. They've lost ground but they're more closely allied with ISIS. I think their main goal will be to prove to the world they're still valid with a large show of force."

In a tag team exchange, Grant nodded and continued where Zane had left off. "Boko Haram has proven over and over that they can adapt and overcome, and fast. Being quick to change tactics and direction to elude us is what makes them hard to defeat. With funding and support from ISIS, they'll be able to set up in neighboring countries. We want to get them now while they're mainly contained in the forest. Our goal for this mission is to capture and kill the group's leader, Shekau. It will take more to completely defeat them, but this will be a damn good start."

"You have a preference on that? Capture or kill?" Brody asked.

The team CO laughed. "You get as far as even laying eyes on Shekau and I'll owe you all a beer. I'll take him any way I can get him. Dead or alive. Use your judgment."

That's the way Brody liked it.

Grant glanced around the room. "We start moving Alpha unit out immediately. Bravo and Charlie will follow tomorrow in the helos just before sunrise. We want the cover of darkness but not to make them suspicious we're planning a full out assault."

Which was exactly what they were doing.

"I suggest everyone get some sleep now while you can," the CO added.

He was right. Once they hit the ground tomorrow, Brody's team would have to move by foot through not only dense, but possibly booby-trapped and mined forest.

Likely they'd have to cool their heels waiting until a truck left camp, in which case they could take turns resting once they were set up.

He only hoped it wouldn't be too long of a wait. Brody didn't want Bravo unit hiding in that forest just a couple of klicks from the camp for too long. He didn't trust the joint forces' troops to not accidentally give their position away or worse, trigger one of the booby traps or mines and blow themselves up.

At least the troops wouldn't be alone. Jon and Chris would remain with Bravo unit in the forest, while Zane and Dawson accompanied Alpha unit on the road.

Thom, Rocky and Brody would be the ones to go after the truck. A smaller team would be less likely to be detected . . . or trip a landmine.

Meanwhile, Grant would orchestrate it all from the command post.

The door swung open and every eye in the room turned toward it. There were maps and sensitive material scattered all over the meeting room. Things that shouldn't be seen by the wrong eyes.

Considering that for now they were still lying about this being a training and not an assault, that included pretty much everyone not in the room.

Mack stopped dead in the doorway and cringed. "Sorry I'm late. Transport issues."

Jaw tight, the CEO said, "Close the door."

Once it was closed, the tension in the room eased up a bit.

Grant nodded to Mack. "I'm glad you made it. They told me you had some trouble getting in."

"Yeah, you could say that." Mack snorted.

The CO glanced at Brody. "Cassidy, brief Mack on the plan. He'll be on Charlie team with you. Everyone else, make sure your kits are packed and get some rest. I need you on the flight line by zero-three-thirty."

Brody stifled a groan. There wasn't much chance of him sleeping unless he drugged himself. But he had to be careful about that since they were mustering early.

He'd decide what to do about sleeping later. Right now, he had Mack's surprise visit to deal with.

As the room slowly emptied, Brody turned to Mack. "I didn't know you were gonna be here."

"I asked for a transfer out of my unit."

"What? Why?" The moment the question was out of his mouth, Brody realized why. "Speedy?"

"Yeah. I feel like a fucking pussy but I couldn't go back there." He raised dark eyes to meet Brody's. "I'm not afraid."

"I know." Brody nodded.

"I mean it, dude. I will gladly die on this op—"

Brody held up one hand. "Mack, I believe you. I get it. You go back to Fallujah and you'll spend the whole time second-guessing what you did that day. What you might have done differently. The *what ifs*, not to mention the guilt, it's too much of a distraction. You'd be putting yourself and your team in danger."

Mack nodded, silent. He drew in a breath and let

it out. "Thanks for understanding."

"No problem. Now let's go over this plan so I can get some fucking sleep. Tomorrow starts at zero-dark-thirty and our workday isn't gonna end until we take out the target."

Mack treated Brody to a half-hearted smile. "That sounds pretty good to me."

Brody let out a short huff of a laugh. "It would."

He stood and led the way to the map where he could better explain the plan that would hopefully be the beginning of the end of Boko Haram in Nigeria.

CHAPTER SEVENTEEN

Ashley carried the tray to the bedroom and set it down. As she handed the glass of tea to Miss Eleanor, she asked, "So, have you heard from Brody?"

The older woman reached for the glass and glanced at Ashley. "Yes, he called."

"He did?" She did her best to act casually as her heart thundered and her mind raced. He could call home but not call her?

What the hell?

"Yes. He told me there were muffins left in the fridge. Can you get me one?"

Ashley tried to calm herself. "No, Miss Eleanor. That was a few days ago. You ate them all. Remember?"

Horrible as it sounded, Ashley was relieved the

woman's mind seemed to be slipping just a bit and that Brody really hadn't called the house but not her.

"Yes, of course I remember eating them, I just thought there might be more left." Miss Eleanor, obviously insulted Ashley had insinuated she hadn't remembered, scowled and focused back on the television.

That was fine. Ashley needed to get her emotions back on an even keel. She'd made herself a promise to understand his job and his dedication to it. She'd vowed that when he did get in touch with her— whenever that might be—she'd support him and be understanding.

All of that was easier said then done.

Reading everything about world events that she could get her hands on had turned out to be a mixed bag.

In one respect, it helped her understand everything happening in the world that Brody had to face. On the other hand, it scared the hell out of her that he was out there amid the horrors and the danger.

She changed her guess pretty much nightly as to where she thought he'd been sent.

Currently she was convinced he was helping with the refugees. She liked that theory best since it seemed the safest.

Her other theory was that he'd been called to fight ISIS in Iraq. That was her least comforting scenario. Even thinking of it now, and the grim tally of the group's assassinations, twisted her gut as she carried the tray back to the kitchen.

Safe in Alabama was not at all a comforting place to be. It should be, but it wasn't. Not when the man she'd loved with her whole heart once upon a time—the man who she was doing her best to not love now—was in mortal danger somewhere doing something. All information he couldn't ever tell her.

In the rollercoaster of her emotions, for every high there seemed to be two lows.

Standing in his family's kitchen where she'd spent so many happy hours as a child, she grasped at what little hope she could find. In the next breath she had to think there was no hope for them.

Even if she did pick up her life and follow him to his base, how could she live with him gone all the time? How could she live a life while he kept her in the dark?

The doubt crept in and she wondered if it even mattered what she wanted. Maybe Brody didn't want her in his life.

The ringing of the house phone had Ashley jumping. She leapt for it. If by some miracle it was Brody calling, she wasn't going to miss it.

"Hello?"

"Is this little Ashley answering my momma's phone?"

The voice sounded enough like Brody's it had her heart pounding, but it was clear it wasn't him. "Chris. Hi. It's me."

"Well, I'll be damned. Brody told me he'd seen you. How you been?"

"Good. Um, you talked to Brody?"

"Oh yeah. I was just with him."

"You were? I thought he got called back to duty

. . . or whatever." This military speak was not exactly in her wheelhouse.

Chris laughed. "He did. I'm with him."

"But, wait. I thought you retired." She frowned.

"I did. I, uh, picked up a part-time job. Actually, I'm going to have to get back to work in about two minutes but I wanted to call the family and say hey first."

Her mind working fast, she was trying to figure out how to get more information out of Chris, and hopefully get to talk to Brody too, all within the two minutes he said he had to spend on the phone.

She still hadn't come up with a plan when fumbling on the other extension of the house phone interrupted her.

"Hello?" Miss Eleanor's voice had Ashley ready to stomp her foot in frustration.

"Hey, Grandmother. It's Chris."

"Chris. It's about time you called."

As he laughed, Ashley felt awkward listening in on this private family moment. "Um, I'm going to hang up now. Bye, Chris."

"Bye, Ash."

She wanted to tell him to say hello to Brody for her. She wanted to ask and say so many things, but all she did was hang up the receiver.

Curiosity won out. She ran down the hall and stood by the doorway of Miss Eleanor's room.

Listening to one half of a conversation was always frustrating. Since Ashley was intruding where she didn't belong and violating almost every rule of the good manners Nana had taught her, she probably deserved the frustration.

Finally, after a conversation that yielded not a whole lot in Ashley's opinion, Miss Eleanor hung up the phone, thereby severing the only connection Ashley had to Brody.

Ashley drew in a breath to calm herself and stepped into the bedroom. "So, that was nice of Chris to call."

"Yes, it was."

Since it hadn't been a question that required an in depth answer, Ashley shouldn't be frustrated that Miss Eleanor's reply didn't enlighten her at all.

She tried again. "When I answered the phone in the kitchen, before you picked up the extension in here, he told me he was working a new job. Did he say where?"

Hopefully the inquiry sounded like everyday small talk and not like what it really was—Ashley's desperate attempt to discover where Brody was and if he was in danger.

The other question uppermost in her mind was why Chris could call home from wherever they were but not Brody. She doubted she'd get that answer from Miss Eleanor, but it might be worth a try.

"Wherever he was, the connection got very bad near the end. I could hardly hear him."

"That's too bad." Ashley nodded, though that didn't tell her much. They could be anywhere, in this country even, where there was poor cell phone coverage.

Though the information helped a little bit. If Chris's phone was getting terrible signal, then maybe Brody's phone wasn't any better. It could even be worse depending on the model of the phone and his carrier.

She knew she was likely grasping at straws, but what else had he left her to hold on to?

Not much.

All she had was his promise that they'd talk again, sometime, when she was *feeling better*.

The pendulum of her emotions swung one more time.

Damn man. If she didn't love him so damn much—

Ashley drew in a breath. Crap. She loved him.

CHAPTER EIGHTEEN

"Alpha unit is in position." Zane's voice came over the comm, funneled directly into Brody's ear.

Brody's T-shirt beneath his body armor was soaked with sweat from the trek, not to mention the oppressive African heat.

He flicked a bead of sweat off his forehead before it ran into his eye and obscured his vision. Besides that there wasn't much he could do about the situation.

"Bravo unit in position," Chris's report followed.

Rocky's sit rep was next. "Charlie unit in— fuck!"

Brody yanked his gaze from the access road leading into the target's camp, to Rocky, in position and also flat on his belly to Brody's right.

"Repeat, Charlie unit?" Grant's question was not

Brody's top priority as he saw what was happening just a couple of yards from him.

Rocky seemed to be in a staring contest with a long green snake barely ten inches from his face.

Farther from the danger of the situation while positioned just to Brody's left, Thom whispered, "Holy shit."

Brody could relate.

The team had made it on foot through miles of dense forest, which took far longer than it should have as they watched for traps and mines.

Based on the deeply worn tire tracks, they'd located the camp and the main access point where the trucks would come and go, but remained far enough away they wouldn't be heard or spotted.

With two men set up along the narrow path, a gap, and then two more men, Charlie unit had positioned themselves to flank the enemy once they left camp and exposed themselves.

The team's next battle should have been against the targets unlucky enough to drive a truck out of that camp. Now it seemed Brody's team would also have to face off against snakes.

Mack, next to Rocky, slowly let go of his rifle and reached down.

Moving fast and with precision, Mack snatched the snake with one hand and sliced off its head with the knife he'd grabbed with the other.

"Command to Charlie unit. Report!" There was more than a little stress evident in Grant's repeated question as it filtered into Brody's ear.

Rocky let out a visible breath of relief as the snake lay in two parts in front of him. "Okay, yeah.

Charlie unit in position."

"You sure about that, Charlie unit?" Grant asked sounding relieved.

Brody figured it was best if he stepped in and finished the report while Rocky caught his breath. "Charlie unit in position. Holding and awaiting movement."

"Roger, Charlie. Out."

There was a click as Grant switched off the open communications, at which point Rocky let out a string of mumbled cusses.

After he'd apparently gotten it all out of his system, Rocky glanced at Mack. "Thanks, dude."

Eyes again focused on the wooded path through the scope of his weapon, Mack answered, "Anytime."

"Not a snake person?" Brody whispered, smiling as he too focused on the path leading to the enemy camp.

After a snort, Rocky said, "Nope."

"I had a couple of snakes growing up. That one was a beauty. Shame I had to kill it." Mack's offering up personal details was so unlike him, it had Brody glancing his direction.

Rocky lifted a brow in reaction as he too shot Mack a look. "Yeah. Real shame."

Smiling, Brody went back to watching and waiting.

Out of his field of vision, Thom sighed. "Well, at least that was exciting."

Brody understood the man's frustration. They had to be prepared for what could be a long wait for the target to decide to leave. It could be hours, if not days.

Or maybe not . . . the sound of an engine and something big breaking through the trees had all eyes focused on the path.

Brody clicked the communicator to life. "This is Charlie unit. We have movement."

"Roger that," Grant responded from the command post. Alpha and Bravo units, stand by."

Brody was aware of both Zane and Chris acknowledging the order while he kept his focus glued to the path.

It was like the old days. Before Chris had retired. Before Zane and Jon had turned in their separation papers.

Adrenaline pumped through Brody's veins. He was in the zone, primed and ready to take that truck or die trying. Though hopefully not. His dying could fuck up the mission.

It was a good plan. If the leaders were actually in this camp and hadn't gone underground, this attack could take out the heads of this organization.

With any hope, just like the snake they'd encountered, if they cut off the head, the rest would fall.

"Hold steady," he hissed.

The team didn't respond. They didn't have to. They'd been well trained. Rehearsed and re-rehearsed until every action was rote. Until muscle memory took over and freed up the mind to deal with more important things.

The truck, painted green camouflage to blend with the forest, broke through the trees and into view.

Brody had a clear bead on the driver but he didn't take the shot. That wasn't the plan.

All hell would break loose if the target knew they were being fired upon. But if the truck simply broke down, as trucks tended to do, they wouldn't think much of it.

They needed to know how many vehicles and how many men they were dealing with, and to do that the team had to hold back and wait for them to get closer and be more exposed on the path.

Brody and Thom were set up closer to the truck with Rocky and Mack farther back and slightly to the side. From their cover amidst the foliage, the team would have the vehicle and its inhabitants surrounded.

A second truck emerged from the trees.

Two. Double the challenge, but still doable. Once the lead truck was disabled with a well-placed bullet in the tire, the second would be blocked from moving forward by the first until they changed the flat.

If all went as planned, the men would unload and move together to investigate the flat tire, giving Brody's team not only a headcount but also a clear shot at them all, all at once, in one easy to manage group.

Of course, the targets would eventually set up guards before they fixed the flat, so time was of the essence.

Brody's team would have to use the element of surprise to their advantage. They had to hit before the group got organized.

The trucks rumbled along the path, getting closer

to Brody. When no other vehicle emerged from the break in the woods, Brody reported, "Two enemy vehicles. Unknown number of targets. Taking out the tire."

With the sound of the shot muffled by a suppressor, the bad guys had no clue why their truck was suddenly listing to one side.

The convoy came to a stop almost directly in front of the team's position.

Men piled out of the back of two vehicles, speaking fast and loud as they all moved to the one side of the truck to inspect the flat tire.

That was their fatal mistake.

It was over in under a minute.

Not a surprise, really. Usually firefights never lasted as long in real life as they did in the movies.

It was one of Brody's biggest pet peeves when trying to enjoy an action flick.

Today, most of the ten men who'd left the safety of their camp hadn't had time to raise their weapons before the bullets they never saw coming had taken them out.

Brody couldn't feel too bad about that. One glance showed the targets were all armed to the teeth. Automatic weapons. Handguns. Grenades. Knives. Even a couple of machetes.

While surveying the sheer amount of firepower, Brody said, "We need to clear these weapons."

Thom bent to retrieve one of the M16s. "I guess we'll put it all in back of the good truck for now and deal with disposing of them later."

"Good idea." Brody agreed for multiple reasons.

They couldn't risk the noise of destroying the

weapons here and now but more than that, if they got into a firefight when they hit camp, having the extra weapons and ammo could come in very handy.

Mack, the Catholic among them, crossed himself as he stood over the bodies littering the ground.

Brody understood Mack's reverence.

These men at their feet had been living, breathing humans just moments ago. But they had also been terrorists. They'd pledged fealty to a militant organization who killed, kidnapped and raped those who couldn't defend themselves, all because they didn't believe in the same things.

Judging by the patterns of recent movements and behavior, these men were very likely on their way to attack one of the nearby villages. That village was safe . . . for now.

Brody stood nearby, evaluating the results of a couple of dozen rounds delivered by the weapons of four well-trained men as his teammate finished his silent prayer.

Bending to grab one of the rifles, Rocky shook his head. "More than half of these are ours."

By *ours* Rocky meant the weapons in the hands of the enemy were U.S. made assault rifles, probably the ones meant to arm their allies.

Obviously the days were long gone when the only weapons the bad guys could get their hands on were old Russian leftovers from the conflicts in the 1980s.

Mack turned to the group. "When I was in Fallujah, we learned from the Iraqi authorities that they lost weapons and Humvees when ISIS took

Mosul. I guess this is proof it's being used to supply Boko Haram."

Rocky mumbled a cuss as Mack continued, "The north-south axis to Libya is one of the main supply routes and it's pretty much an open road right now."

"Then we need to shut it down." The determination was clear in Thom's voice.

"And decimate Boko Haram," Rocky added.

"Then we'd better get moving." Brody clicked his communicator to deliver the report. "Charlie to Command. Ten tangos neutralized and we liberated two large presents for y'all."

"Good job, Charlie team. Hold position. Alpha and Bravo, move in."

After Grant barked his orders, Brody turned to the team. "Guess we'd better see about changing this tire if we're gonna use both trucks."

Rocky cocked one brow. "Or we could just use one."

Mack rolled his eyes. "Jeez. I'll change the frigging tire, city boy. Wouldn't want you to get your hands dirty."

"I am not a city boy." Rocky's dark brows drew low in a frown.

Mack let out a snort as he slung his weapon over one shoulder and moved to the back of the truck where a spare tire was mounted. "Whatever you say, Jersey boy."

"Come on, guys. Back me up here." Rocky glanced at Brody and Thom for help.

Brody lifted his shoulder, following the argument even as he kept an eye on the path behind the trucks so they didn't get snuck up on. "You are a Yankee."

Thom, weapon up as he also surveyed the forest around them, laughed softly. "I'm a Yankee too, but I know how to change a tire."

"Motherfuck—" Rocky pressed his lips into a thin unhappy-looking line and shook his head. "I know how to change a damn tire. I just thought we only needed one truck. That was the original plan."

Mack shook his head. "We should use both. Ten men and two trucks left. It won't raise an alarm if that's what comes back."

Brody nodded. "Agreed. Two of us in the front of each of the trucks, and then three troops from Bravo unit in the back of both."

Mack glanced at the bodies on the ground. "Of course, we're gonna have to put on their clothes or the perimeter guards will notice that it's not their men coming back in those trucks."

"I had a bad feeling that was gonna be the plan." Gazing down at the bloodied clothing, Rocky sighed.

"Bravo should be here soon. They'll move quicker since we already marked and cleared the path for them," Brody guessed.

Rocky glanced at Mack, in the midst of spinning off the lug nuts on the truck's flat tire, and then at Brody and Thom, both watching the woods with weapons raised.

Swinging his gun over his shoulder, Rocky mumbled, "Crap. I guess I'd better get started on our new wardrobe."

CHAPTER NINETEEN

"So I glance over and Rocky is literally face to face with this huge snake that I swear is looking him right in the eye, like they were in some sort of staring contest." Thom's recount of the story to the guys back on base got more animated with each telling, though Brody had to admit it had been pretty funny. "I swear, dude, this snake was like six inches away from the tip of Rocky's nose."

Eyes wide, Jon glanced at Rocky. "What the fuck did you do?"

Brody laughed. "Probably shit his pants."

Rocky frowned. "Did not. And let's see how you'd react."

Thom wasn't about to let the story go unfinished just because Brody and Rocky were bickering. He launched into the next part, saying, "So he was in the middle of checking in at the time. So command is freaking out on the radio because all they hear is Rocky cursing and then dead air."

Grant rolled his eyes. "I wasn't freaking out, but I was starting to think my star team—the ringers I hand-picked and flew in just for this freaking op—had gotten ambushed."

"Aw, we're your stars? That's nice." Brody grinned, teasing Grant.

Grant cocked a brow. "Don't let it go to your head."

Undeterred, Thom forged ahead. "So this is the best part. Mack reaches over, as calm as anything. You know, as if this shit happens to him everyday. He snatches the snake, lops off its head with his KA-BAR and then goes back to manning his rifle."

"It was no big deal." Mack shrugged. "But that species is deadly so if it had bit him, *that* would have been a big deal."

Rocky let out a visible shudder. "Ugh, I hate snakes."

"We all have our little quirks." Grant smiled.

Brody laughed. "Yeah, you should see Chris scream and run away like a little girl if he sees a wasp. It's pretty funny . . . Where is he, anyway?"

Jon lifted his hand. "That's on me. We left a small contingency from Bravo unit at the camp to conduct a final sweep for hidden weapons before they destroyed the cache."

Grant nodded. "And, Shekau wasn't among those in the camp, but chances are he was there at one time. If he left any intel behind, I told Chris that I want it."

Brody glanced at the time.

The main force had been back for long enough he'd expect Chris and his team to be walking in any moment. But in the back of his mind remained the fact that anything could happen. The damn weapons could be booby-trapped.

Unlike Jon and Zane, Chris had been away from active duty for long enough he could have lost his edge.

Brody couldn't stop himself from asking, "Have they checked in?"

Grant raised a brow. "You worried?"

Brody hesitated long enough that Grant tipped his head toward the door. "Let's go to the JOC and check. I'll be interested to find out if they found anything myself."

Brody followed Grant. Whoever was manning the Joint Operations Center would have the latest situation report from Chris.

Once he knew what was happening, Brody could get himself some chow and then catch a few winks. But until he knew Chris was all right, he wouldn't be able to rest easy.

The CO was in the operations center when they arrived. He glanced up when they walked in. "Good job with the trucks, Cassidy."

"Thank you, sir."

Grant stepped forward. "What's the latest from Bravo?"

"They saw a squirter heading out the back of camp and into the woods. Before he could disappear, your brother took off after him." The CO directed the last part of the comment to Brody.

"Has he reported in?" Brody asked.

"Not yet. But when Jones called in thirty minutes ago, he said Cassidy was running full out after the guy. I wouldn't expect him to give up the chase to take the time to call in."

"They let him go alone?" Brody's eyes widened.

"Jones said that as your brother was taking off into the woods, he told him to take over and finish the job."

Chris was forty. He was in good shape but damn, for this kind of job he was an old man.

Brody could run full out for a good long while after a target, but could Chris?

Hell, more than age was the danger. Chris, out there alone on the tangos' home turf, could get led straight into an ambush.

He dragged in a breath and realized how tight his chest felt as worry pressed down on him like a lead weight.

Brody was getting a good education in exactly how badly being on this side of the waiting and the worrying sucked.

"You still worried?" Grant asked.

"Yes."

"Why?"

Why? "He's alone."

Grant lifted a brow. "Yes, but he made that choice. Retired or not, Chris is still a highly trained, combat-experienced, well-armed DEVGRU operative. You have to trust he knows what he's doing."

And they'd all been prepared for this kind of scenario and blah, blah, blah, so many other reasons why Brody shouldn't be concerned, but the fact remained, he was.

"But he's also my brother." Brody made eye contact with Grant and saw him react to the statement.

"He was your brother when you were on the team together too. He's been in sticky situations before. I never saw you worry like this."

"I know." Brody bobbed his head, accepting the truth of what Grant said.

"So what changed over the past two years since he retired?" Grant asked.

"It's closer to three years and I honestly don't know."

But Brody suspected. Two days with his first and only love and he'd gone soft.

The question remained, what could he do about it and what the hell was he going to do with himself and this overwhelming weight of worry about Chris?

He supposed he'd just have to deal with it until his damn brother, who'd put himself into danger, got himself out of it again.

CHAPTER TWENTY

Ashley had been asleep when her cell phone woke her.

True to form for her, at least for the past few days, when any phone rang anywhere she jumped to grab it.

Still half asleep and in the dark, she dove for the phone that was lit up on the nightstand.

The unfamiliar area code on the display had her frowning. Her tired brain reasoned hazily that it could be a telemarketer. The bastards had begun to bother people by cell phone now instead of just on the house phone.

But it had to be the middle of the night, if not really early in the morning, judging by the lack of even a glow of sunlight coming through her window. Even telemarketers didn't call this early.

It didn't matter. There was no way she was going to let the call go to voicemail. It could be Brody.

Ashley hit the button to answer. "Hello?"

"Ash? It's me."

She listened to the nuances in the voice delivering those three short words and knew whom it was without having to ask. "Brody."

His mumbled cuss came through the line. "I woke you up. I'm so sorry. I guess I didn't figure the time zones right."

"No. It's fine. I'm awake." No way was she letting him hang up just because he felt bad he'd woken her.

She'd gladly miss an entire night of sleep to be able to talk to Brody, especially now when he was God only knew where doing things she could barely imagine.

"How are you?" She had hoped and prayed he'd call but now that he was actually on the line she couldn't come up with a thing to say besides inane small talk.

He let out a short laugh. "I'm fine."

Something was wrong. She could hear it in his voice. "Is everything all right?"

He hesitated a beat before she heard his intake of breath and then his sigh. If she hadn't been so tuned in to him, listening as closely as the phone connection would allow, she might have missed those telltale sounds before he finally answered, "Uh . . . yeah."

Whatever it was, he couldn't tell her. She felt it to her bones that he wanted to but he couldn't—and she'd gone and put pressure on him, making him feel even more badly about it.

That was what she had done when she'd grilled him before he left from his leave. Then, she had wanted to know where he was going, when she'd see him again, when he'd be able to call her, but he couldn't tell her. So she'd cried and he'd felt bad.

Time for her to start acting like the understanding person she'd sworn to herself she'd be if ever given another chance with Brody.

Ashley drew in a breath and launched into a diversion that would hopefully cheer him up, no matter what was wrong. "So we had some excitement at your house today."

"Yeah? What happened?" he asked.

"A mouse decided he wanted a piece of your grandmother's toast while she was sleeping. He crawled right up on her nightstand and was sitting on her plate nibbling on the crust when she woke up. You would have thought the house was on fire with as loud as Miss Eleanor screamed."

This time Brody's laugh didn't sound bitter. It was a genuine reaction to the story she'd relayed. Ashley smiled that whatever was wrong wherever he was, she could still make him laugh by providing a little piece of home.

"What did you do?" he asked.

"Well, not a whole lot. By the time I got to her room that mouse had high-tailed it out of there and was long gone. Of course, I had to spend the rest of the day conducting anti-mouse activities. Setting up traps. Calling your father to ask him to bring home poison. Googling, literally searching for a better mouse trap on the internet."

"That's funny." He laughed again and Ashley's heart warmed.

Was this how all those people with loved ones in the military dealt with it? Ignore the elephant in the room—that the person on the other end of the line could be hurt or killed any moment—and just go on like normal?

Hearing him laugh made this charade more than worth it. And she had to admit pretending everything was fine was making her feel better too—at least for the moment. She had no doubt the second she hung up with him the weight of fear and worry would be back.

She wanted to ask so many questions. She wanted to apologize.

Instead, she wracked her brain for more little tidbits of home to amuse him. "So I'm kind of going to cheat tomorrow at work. I convinced Nana to come visiting Miss Eleanor since they haven't seen each other in weeks."

"So the two old ladies can keep each other busy and leave you alone, you mean?"

She heard the amusement in his voice and joked, "Don't you let Nana hear you calling her old or she'll never bake your favorite muffins specially for you again."

"Okay. I won't."

"But yes, that was the general idea."

After a short chuckle at her admission, he let out another deep sigh, as if the weight of the world was on him.

Again Ashley bit her tongue, not questioning, just waiting.

Finally, he continued, "I really should go."

"I understand. I'm glad you called." She'd done her best to sound upbeat. She even thought it might have worked.

"Me too . . . Ash?"

"Yeah?"

"I love you. You know that, right?"

No, she hadn't known that. Mouth hanging open, her mind reeled.

He loved her how? Like a sister? Like a friend? Like an ex-girlfriend he'd always love but was no longer *in love* with?

This wasn't the time to ask, even with as much as she wanted to. The questions would haunt her. Forget about sleeping again tonight. She knew she'd be wondering long past dawn.

She swallowed away the lump in her throat that his surprise pronouncement had cause. "I love you too."

He drew in an audible breath and let it out again. "I'm gonna go. Bye, Ash."

"Bye." Tears filled her eyes as there was a click on the line.

She'd never heard him sound so down. So listless. Why?

His goodbye had sounded so final. Was he about to go out on some kind of suicide mission he didn't expect to return from and that's why he'd called? Why he'd told her he loved her?

The helplessness was overwhelming and there wasn't a single thing she could do about it except curl in a ball on her bed and cry.

CHAPTER TWENTY-ONE

Rocky watched Brody pace the room. "How long has it been?"

"Too fucking long." His reply was terse. Brody let out a huff of breath. Rocky didn't deserve his bad attitude. "Sorry."

"No worries. I know where you're coming from."

It had to be hours since Chris had taken off after that target.

Hours!

There was only one reason why he wouldn't have radioed in by now.

Two actually—Chris was either captured or dead.

Brody glanced at his watch again. "Five more minutes and I'm walking into that JOC and telling them I'm going out looking for him."

Rocky cocked a brow. "You think they'll let you?"

"Let me?" Brody's eyebrows shot high. "They should have already organized a search. I shouldn't have to ask permission. An operative is out there alone and missing—"

"If and when they do send out a team, I'll go. You're not going." Mack stood in the open doorway.

"I gotta agree." Rocky nodded. "Let the rest of us go but you shouldn't. You're too involved in this."

"But he's my brother."

Mack dipped his head. "Exactly."

While Brody's mouth hung wide as he tried to come up with an argument, Mack continued, "It's the same reason why they don't let surgeons operate on their own family. They're too close to it."

"That's ridiculous. Chris and I used to be on the same team. We've had each other's back in more dangerous situations than this."

"Maybe so," Rocky agreed. "I wasn't there but obviously things worked out fine back then, but can you guarantee you can think clearly right now? You trust yourself to make the best decision for the team, emotions aside?"

Brody drew in a breath to tell Rocky yes, but he couldn't say the word because he wasn't sure.

Things had changed. This felt different. He felt different.

"Fuck." Brody sat heavily in the chair and raised his gaze to the two other men in the room. "I've lost my edge."

Rocky rolled his eyes. "You haven't lost shit. I saw you today when we drove into that camp. You took out one guy in hand-to-hand combat at the same time that you whipped out your sidearm and shot another. It's just this situation. That's all. He's your brother. Cut yourself some slack."

Mack nodded. "A smart operative knows when to fight and he knows when to sit one out."

Brody eyed Mack. The man didn't say a whole hell of a lot but when he did, he usually knew what he was talking about.

Mack had known when to bow out of his team. Known that he had to ask for a transfer or risk not being able to perform.

Maybe Speedy's death had hit Brody harder than he'd thought it had.

Sad to say, but Brody preferred that idea over the alternative. It was easier to swallow that it was the loss of a fellow operative and not his reunion with Ashley that had rattled him.

Though if Brody was honest with himself he'd admit both events were tied together.

It was his feeling his own mortality so keenly, fresh from Speedy's memorial service, that had driven him so quickly into Ashley's arms. Back into that emotional quagmire that had been their relationship since they had been teenagers dancing around each other.

Before they'd finally started dating.

Before they'd broken up.

"A'ight. I'll stay put. But I'm still going to the JOC and demanding they send out a team."

"Mmm, hmm." Rocky nodded. "Or the three of us can go and express our collective concern as experienced operatives and ask the command what their thoughts are."

Brody frowned at Rocky. "Since when are you the diplomat on the team?"

Rocky lifted one brow. "Since you took over being the team's loose canon."

Out of the corner of his eye, Brody saw Mack's lips twitch with a smile.

"Fair enough." Brody let out a sigh and stood. "Let's go."

CHAPTER TWENTY-TWO

Weeks.

It had been weeks since that ominous middle of the night phone call from Brody.

Since then, Ashley had survived one day at a time. Every morning she held her breath as she drove up to the Cassidy's house.

Every day that she arrived and didn't find the family grieving over horrible news was a relief. But the reprieve from worry only lasted a few seconds before Ashley went on alert listening for the sound of the phone or a car in the drive.

There'd been no notice from anyone official in the military, but there also hadn't been any more calls from either Chris or Brody. She knew because she'd asked as often as she thought she could get away with without sounding suspicious.

All of that enormous patience she'd shown during the complete communications drought over the past weeks broke as she pulled her car into the Cassidy's driveway today.

There was a pick-up truck parked there. It wasn't Brody's but it did have a Virginia license plate.

What did that mean? Had someone from Brody's base driven all the way to Alabama to break the bad news to the family in person?

What Ashley didn't know about military protocol far outweighed what she did know. She loved Brody since she'd been a kid, but this was uncharted territory for her.

Not knowing seemed preferable to knowing as she sat shaking in the driver's seat.

If she didn't go inside the house, he could still be all right. If she didn't know for a fact that something bad had happened, then she could still pretend that everything might be fine.

Ashley struggled to breathe as her stomach roiled.

This was ridiculous. She had to go in.

She pulled the key from the ignition, swung open the door and stepped onto the driveway. She slammed the door only to realize she'd forgotten her purse. And she needed the bag with Miss Eleanor's new prescription medications that she'd stopped by the pharmacy to pick up this morning.

Frustrated, Ashley opened the car's door and crawled across the driver's seat to reach the bags on the passenger side.

Now that she'd made the decision to go inside and face the news, good or bad, it seemed she couldn't get there fast enough.

Bag in hand she hurried past the truck, giving it a wide berth. It was ridiculous really, but she didn't want to risk seeing anything inside. What might be in there for her to be afraid of she didn't know but she didn't take any chances

Then she was on the top step by the front door.

Blowing out a big huff of air through her mouth, she reached for the knob and turned.

The moment the door opened she heard it—voices in the kitchen. Male voices. Two of them and she recognized them both.

Nearly sagging to the floor at the sound, Ashley reached for the doorframe and braced her palm against it trying to regulate her breathing before she hyperventilated.

Unless she was hallucinating, they were both there. Both safe.

Chris and Brody were home.

After so much worry, she had to fight tears of relief as she pushed the front door closed. Moving closer to the kitchen she began to be able to decipher words instead of just voices.

The conversation she heard had her pausing before she entered the room.

She heard Chris say, "Just letting you know that I'm fixin' to go to the bathroom. A'ight with you?"

"Fuck you." The tone of Brody's response showed he wasn't pleased with Chris's comment.

"Just didn't want you to get too worried while I'm gone, bro."

"You took off after a tango with no backup and didn't check in with command for hours. I'm not supposed to worry about you?"

"I was a little busy, bro."

"Tracking the squirter. I know. So you said. But the ROE were to neutralize the targets, not track them like you're on a damn hog hunt."

"I'm retired. I work for GAPS now and GAPS is a PMC so your ROEs don't apply to me anymore."

Moving closer, Ashley heard Brody snort at Chris's comment. Meanwhile, half of the conversation, spoken in acronyms she didn't understand, went right over her head.

Chris continued, "Besides, that tango I saw escaping into the trees could easily have led me to another camp. Possibly to where Shekau was hiding. It could have been where those missing schoolgirls were being held. I needed to take the chance."

"He ended up leading you nowhere."

"Yup, but I brought him back alive so command can persuade him to share anything he does know."

Shekau. Missing schoolgirls. Ashley had researched so obsessively over the past weeks, just from hearing those words she could guess where Brody and Chris had been.

Her grandmother would tan her hide if she ever caught her eavesdropping like this, but Ashley also knew Brody and Chris would never share details like this with her so she had no choice.

Still, the guilt began to creep upon her. So did the desire that she'd been away from him for long enough. She wanted to see Brody. Hug him. Feel his arms wrap around her.

"Just don't ever pull that kind of shit—" Brody

stopped mid-sentence when his gaze landed on Ashley after she moved into the open doorway.

"Hi." Ashley had imagined this moment for weeks. Now, in the same room with Brody, she was feeling inexplicably shy.

"Ash. Good God Almighty, you're a sight for sore eyes." Chris pushed himself off the counter he'd been leaning against and came forward.

Before Ashley knew it, she was ensconced in arms of steel and pressed against his hard chest.

"Hi, Chris. It's good to see you too."

When Chris pulled back and finally released her, she turned to find Brody had stepped closer.

The corner of his mouth tipped up in a partial smile. "Hey, Ash."

"Brody." She didn't wait for him to move. She went to him and threw her arms around his neck.

Maybe she shouldn't have, but it wasn't like she hadn't just hugged his brother. Why shouldn't she embrace her childhood friend upon his homecoming?

He squeezed her so tightly it forced the air from her lungs. She wasn't about to complain. He was home and it felt so good to be in his arms.

Through his T-shirt, she felt his heart beating against the cheek she had pressed to his chest. She would be happy to remain right there like that forever, but knew she couldn't.

She pulled back and dared to glance at Chris.

He'd gone back to leaning against the kitchen counter again, but now he wore an amused expression as if he could see right through the sham she'd hoped to perpetrate against the whole family that she and Brody were just friends.

Chris glanced at Brody. "I was wondering what went on here during your last visit home."

The older family members had been so easy to fool. Chris obviously was not.

Still, Ashley tried. "What are you talking about? Nothing—"

"Ash. Stop. I went along with it when we were kids but I'm not doing it anymore. If we're going to be together, my family has to know."

Chris's amused expression gave way to a frown. "When you were kids? You were together back then?"

"Yup." Brody grinned. "Fooled ya, huh?"

Chris mouthed a cuss. "Yeah, you did. But at least now I know why you've been acting so crazy the past few weeks."

Now it was Brody's turn to frown. "I have not."

"Ashley!" Miss Eleanor, her timing impeccably annoying as always, summoned her from the bedroom.

Maybe that was for the best. Ashley could use an excuse to remove herself from Chris's scrutiny. She felt as if he was trying to look deep into her soul and discover all the secrets she'd worked so hard to hide for so many years.

"I'd better go bring this to her." Ashley held up the paper bag containing pill bottles that she'd forgotten was still clutched in her hand.

"A'ight. Hurry back." Brody's smile, so familiar, so sexy, had her stomach twisting.

She didn't answer, opting instead to duck out on the whole embarrassing situation.

"Dude. Ashley? You dog." Chris's comment followed her down the hall and Ashley saw clearly how her plan to leave and avoid embarrassment hadn't worked out so well.

Brody came back at his brother with an annoyed sounding, "Shut up."

A deep chuckle was Chris's only response.

With a sigh, she abandoned worrying about what was happening in the kitchen between the brothers and entered the bedroom. "Good morning, Miss Eleanor."

"About time you got here. Help me up. I want to get dressed."

"Okay, but why don't you stay comfortable in bed and have your breakfast and take your pills first?"

"Because I'm having my breakfast in the kitchen with my grandsons. That's why."

"Grandmother has told me how she foiled your evil plan to keep her bedridden. And how now she's walking all over the place." Brody's comment had Ashley turning to see him standing in the doorway.

"Her condition was what was keeping her bedridden. Not me."

Ashley could have taken the time to explain to Brody, and to Miss Eleanor yet again, how the blood pressure medicine the doctor had prescribed had been causing the vertigo. How now that they'd gotten that regulated and weaned her to a lower dose of the blood thinner, it was safe for her to walk around the house without the danger of falling and without her bruising anytime she brushed against anything.

Instead of all of that, Ashley just sighed. "I'd be happy to help you get dressed so you can eat in the kitchen."

Brody smiled at her show of tolerance. "Well, hurry up, both of you. Nana just got here."

"Nana's here?" Ashley frowned. She'd left Nana happily sipping sweet tea and reading the newspaper on the front porch about an hour ago. "She didn't tell me she was coming today."

"Apparently, Grandmother called Nana this morning to tell her I had returned from war and had specially requested her muffins." Brody crossed his arms and cocked a brow as he leveled an accusatory gaze on Miss Eleanor.

The older woman didn't flinch. "What? You don't want muffins? Fine. More for me."

Ashley couldn't help but laugh. "All right, you two. What's done is done. Brody, can you please ask Nana to make a fresh pot of coffee so we can all have it with her muffins?"

"Yes, ma'am." Cocky grin firmly in place, Brody pushed off the doorway he'd been leaning against.

Ashley ignored him and turned to the woman currently trying to get out of bed without any assistance. She stepped forward, not daring to help without being asked, but ready in case she needed it.

It was hard for Ashley to wrap her head around everything that had happened in such a short time. Both boys being home and safe. Nana back in the Cassidy kitchen again. Miss Eleanor up and around and her usual bossy self. Brody revealing to Chris that they had been, and would be again, together.

It had been a long time since Ashley had felt this contented. If she could figure out exactly what being *together* with Brody meant, today would be pretty much perfect.

CHAPTER TWENTY-THREE

"So I figure we should talk." Brody knew it was true even if he'd rather kiss than talk.

Hell, more than just kiss, since the weeks without Ashley had done a lot to raise his hunger to feel her sweet body beneath his again.

But if this thing between them was going to have any chance of working, they needed to communicate.

Since he wasn't all that good in that department, it meant he'd have to work extra hard to make sure he didn't screw things up. Messing up with Ashley a second time was the last thing he intended to do.

He had to believe that if things were settled between them, he'd get his edge back. He'd be able to go on a mission confident she was okay at home. That she'd be there waiting for him when he got back.

The big question in his mind was if that was what she wanted too. That, and what they were going to do about the miles between her life in Alabama and his in Virginia.

He wrestled his spinning mind back to Ashley, realizing she'd been quiet. Reaching out, he captured her hand in his. "Something wrong?"

She laced her fingers through his. "I'm not sure I want to talk."

He frowned, confused by her answer. "Why not?"

"Things are going so well. I'm afraid talking might mess it all up."

Brody had to admit that it had been a pretty great day, starting with Nana's muffins hot from the oven and ending with him and Chris surrounded by family eating the welcome home supper of chicken and dumplings she'd insisted on cooking for them.

And of course there had been spending the day with Ashley. Even after being together all day, he'd snuck out of the house to see her tonight.

Hopefully that would be the final time and after this there would be no more sneaking around. He would be able to proudly tell his family he and Ashley were more than friends. But he wanted to talk to her first to define what exactly they were as a couple before making some grand revelation to his family.

Of course, there was a part of him that really enjoyed her shock when he crawled through her bedroom window after dark. Maybe he'd keep doing it just for fun.

He pulled her closer, hoping to alleviate her concern. "Our talking can't ruin anything. I promise."

She paused for long enough before she spoke that he didn't think she was going to say anything at all. "Why didn't you call me right away when you got home?"

A fair enough question for a person not used to military transportation. "Communications were horrible while I was traveling. Then by the time we got back and I'd finished doing everything I needed to do it was already getting too late to call."

"I wouldn't have minded."

"I know, but I woke you up once in the middle of the night. I didn't want to do it again. So when I got home I talked to Chris. We decided to drive right here and surprise y'all."

Flying commercial with Jon and Zane had gotten Chris home a full four days before Brody, whose life and travel were dictated by the whim of the military.

Zane had gotten the three of them bumped up to first class, to boot. But the good news was, since Chris had gotten to spend those days with Darci, he was more than willing and able to come with Brody on this trip home without causing havoc with the girlfriend.

Brody's parents were surprised, all right, as he and Chris came busting into the house before dawn.

One glance at her face told him she was holding in something. She used to get the same expression when she was little and had a question she wanted to ask but was afraid to.

He brushed one hand across her cheek. "What you thinking about, darlin'?"

"That phone call. The one in the middle of the night."

"I'll be more careful about the time zones from now on. Promise." Though that call was less about his math being faulty than his grasping for something to hold on to for those hours that Chris was technically missing.

It didn't matter Chris was fine the entire time he'd been in pursuit of the tango, since Brody hadn't known that.

"It wasn't the time." Ashley shook her head. "What did you mean . . . you said . . . at the end when you said you loved me." She drew in a breath and finally raised her gaze to meet his.

He lifted one shoulder. "I do."

An adorable crease formed between her brows. "But how? Like how you love Chris? Or Nana?"

She was perfectly serious and this was an important conversation, but Brody couldn't help the laugh that burst from him. "No. I definitely don't want to do to Chris or Nana the things I want to do to you."

"So it's just about sex." She tried to put on a brave face, but her disappointment was pretty clear in her tone.

"No, Ash. It's not. This is new to me too . . . and at the same time old, which I won't deny is kind of strange. I've loved you since I was little, then I loved you differently when we got older. Now . . ." He shrugged again. "I'm ready to see where this thing between us can go. If you are."

Brody didn't usually suffer from insecurity but today he sure was. He'd bared his heart to her before, had offered her his name and his life, for as long as he was lucky enough to have it, and she'd turned it all down.

Her answer was to lean in and plant a big kiss on his lips. He'd take that response any day.

He let himself enjoy the feel of her lips against his for a good long while. Still, the fact remained they weren't done talking.

He broke the kiss and leaned his forehead against hers. "We'll work it out. Take things slow. I'll come home when I can. You visit when you can."

"Okay." She nodded against his head.

He wasn't going to make the same mistake as last time by asking her to abandon her life there and move. That wouldn't be fair to her or to Nana, who'd no doubt gotten used to having Ashley around again.

Maybe the answer was simpler than he thought. "And you know, I won't be in the military forever—"

"No." She shook her head so adamantly he had to pull back a few inches to give her space. "I would never ever ask you to get out of the military just for me. Or for us. Your job is too important—"

The complete change in her attitude about his being in the military was a shock, but he nodded. "Okay. We'll deal with it. Together."

177

It wasn't going to be easy, but they'd just have to make the most of the time they had for now.

Then, eventually, maybe he would go shopping for another diamond ring. He had to believe her answer would be different this time. They were different people now.

Hell, he was a different person than he'd been just a month ago before coming home to the shock of finding her standing at the front door.

"Brody?"

"Yeah."

"Can we be done talking for now?" As she raised her big warm eyes to meet his, she ran one finger down his chest.

Her hand landed at the waistband of his pants, which gave him a pretty good idea of what she wanted to do instead of talk.

Brody could be completely on board with that plan. Smiling, he said, "Yeah, we can."

If you enjoyed Loved by a SEAL, *please leave a review and look for more in the Hot SEALs series in eBook, print & audio. Never miss a new release. Sign up at catjohnson.net/news to receive notice.*

Hot SEALs

Night with a SEAL
Saved by a SEAL
SEALed at Midnight
Kissed by a SEAL
Protected by a SEAL
Loved by a SEAL
Tempted by a SEAL
Wed to a SEAL

For more titles by Cat visit **CatJohnson.net**

ABOUT THE AUTHOR

Cat Johnson is a *New York Times* bestseller and the author of the *USA Today* bestselling titles *Saved by a SEAL* and *Kissed by a SEAL (Hot SEALs)* and *One Night with a Cowboy (Oklahoma Nights)*. She writes contemporary romance featuring sexy alpha heroes. Known for her unique marketing and research practices, she has sponsored pro bull riders, owns a collection of camouflage and western wear for book signings, and a fair number of her friends/book consultants wear combat or cowboy boots for a living. She writes both full length and shorter works.

Join the mailing list at **catjohnson.net/news**

Made in the USA
San Bernardino, CA
22 September 2015